PUFFIN BOOKS

Paul Jennings was born in England in 1943 and emigrated to Australia aged six. The trip for the family cost ten pounds – the Australian government paid the rest of the fare in those days.

Paul taught disabled and socially deprived children for six years and then worked as a speech therapist. He later lectured in special education before his appointment as Senior Lecturer in Language and Literature at the Warrnambool Institute, where he worked for ten years before becoming a full-time writer in 1989.

Paul's stories are funny, weird, and wacky with surprising endings. He wants all children to have their noses in the same books and reluctant readers to discover that reading is fun. 'Books are fantastic. That's what I want my readers to think.'

Since *Unreal!* was published in 1985, Paul's books have sold over six million copies. He has won many 'Children's Choice' awards and in January 1995 was awarded the Medal of the Order of Australia for Services to Children's Literature.

PAUL JENNINGS

Unmentionable!

PUFFIN BOOKS

PUFFIN BOOKS

Published by the Penguin Group
Penguin Books Ltd, 80 Strand, London WC2R 0RL, England
Penguin Putnam Inc., 375 Hudson Street, New York, New York 10014, USA
Penguin Books Australia Ltd, 250 Camberwell Road, Camberwell, Victoria 3124, Australia
Penguin Books Canada Ltd, 10 Alcorn Avenue, Toronto, Ontario, Canada M4V 3B2
Penguin Books India (P) Ltd, 11 Community Centre, Panchsheel Park, New Delhi – 110 017, India
Penguin Books (NZ) Ltd, Cnr Rosedale and Airborne Roads, Albany, Auckland, New Zealand
Penguin Books (South Africa) (Pty) Ltd, 24 Sturdee Avenue, Rosebank 2196, South Africa

Penguin Books Ltd, Registered Offices: 80 Strand, London WC2R 0RL, England

www.penguin.com

First published by Penguin Books Australia 1991
First published in Great Britain in Puffin Books 1992
21

Typeset in Berkeley

Printed in England by Clays Ltd, St Ives plc

British Library Cataloguing in Publication Data
A CIP catalogue record for this book is available from the British Library

ISBN-13: 978-0-14-037104-8

www.greenpenguin.co.uk

Penguin Books is committed to a sustainable future
for our business, our readers and our planet.
The book in your hands is made from paper
certified by the Forest Stewardship Council.

For Bruce Jeans
who encouraged me to write my first book

Contents

Ice Maiden

I just wouldn't go anywhere near a redhead.

Now don't get me wrong and start calling me a hairist or something like that. Listen to what I have to say, then make up your mind.

It all started with Mr Mantolini and his sculptures.

They were terrific, were Mr Mantolini's frozen statues. He carved them out of ice and stood them in the window of his fish shop which was over the road from the pier. A new ice carving every month.

Sometimes it would be a beautiful peacock with its tail fanned out. Or maybe a giant fish thrashing itself to death on the end of a line. One of my favourites was a kangaroo with a little joey peering out of her pouch.

It was a bit sad really. On the first day of every month Mr Mantolini would throw the old statue out the back into an alley. Where it would melt and trickle away into a damp patch on the ground.

A new statue would be in the shop window. Sparkling blue and silver as if it had been carved from a solid chunk of the Antarctic shelf.

Every morning on my way to school, I would stop to stare at his statue. And on the first of the month I would be there after school to see the new one. I couldn't bear to go around the back and watch yesterday's sculpture melt into the mud.

'Why do you throw them out?' I asked one day.

Mr Mantolini shrugged. 'You live. You die,' he said.

Mr Mantolini took a deep breath. Now he was going to ask me something. The same old thing he had asked every day for weeks. 'My cousin Tony come from Italy. Next month. You take to school. You friend. My cousin have red hair. You like?'

I gave him my usual answer. 'Sorry,' I said. 'I won't be able to.' I couldn't tell him that it was because I hated red hair. I didn't want to hurt his feelings.

He just stood there without saying anything. He was disappointed in me because we were friends. He knew how much I liked his ice statues and he always came out to talk to me about them. 'You funny boy,' he said. He shook his head and walked inside.

I thought I saw tears in Mr Mantolini's eyes. I knew
I had done the wrong thing again. And I was sorry.
But I didn't want a redhead for a mate.

2

I felt guilty and miserable all day. But after school
I cheered up a bit. It was the first of September.
There would be a new ice statue in the window. It
was always something to look forward to.

I hurried up to the fish shop and stared through
the glass. I couldn't believe what I saw. The ice
statue of a girl. It reminded me of one of those Greek
sculptures that you see in museums. It had long
tangled hair. And smiling lips. Its eyes sparkled like
frozen diamonds. I tell you this. That ice girl was
something else. She was fantastic.

'You're beautiful,' I said under my breath. 'Beautiful.'

Of course she was only a statue. She couldn't see
or hear me. She was just a life-sized ice maiden,
standing among the dead fish in the shop window.
She was inside a glass fridge which kept her cold.
Her cheeks were covered with frost.

I stood there for ages just gawking at her. I know
it was stupid. I would have died if anyone knew

what I was thinking. How embarrassing. I had a crush on a piece of ice.

Every day after that, I visited the fish shop. I was late for school because of the ice maiden. I filled every spare minute of my time standing outside the window. It was as if I was hypnotised. The ice maiden's smile seemed to be made just for me. Her outstretched hand beckoned. 'Get real,' I said to myself. 'What are you doing here? You fool.' I knew I was mad but something kept drawing me back to the shop.

Mr Mantolini wouldn't meet my gaze. He was cross with me.

I pretended the ice girl was my friend. I told her my secrets. Even though she was made of ice, I had this silly feeling that she understood.

Mr Mantolini saw me watching her. But he didn't come outside. And whenever I went inside to buy fish for Mum, he scurried out the back and sent his assistant to serve me.

3

The days passed. Weeks went by. The ice maiden smiled on and on. She never changed. The boys thought I was nuts standing there gawking at a lump of ice. But she had this power over me – really. Kids started to tease me. 'He's in love,' said a girl called Simone. I copped a lot of teasing at school but still I kept gazing in that window.

As the days went by I grew sadder and sadder. I wanted to take the ice girl home. I wanted to keep her for ever. But once she was out of her glass cage, in the warm air, her smiling face would melt and drip away.

I dreaded the first of October. When Mr Mantolini would take the ice maiden and dump her in the alley. To be destroyed by the warm rays of the sun.

On the last day of September I waited until Mr Mantolini was serving in the shop. 'You can't throw her out,' I yelled. 'She's too lovely. She's real. You mustn't. You can't.' I was nearly going to say, 'I love her,' but that would have been stupid.

Mr Mantolini looked at me and shrugged. 'You live. You die,' he said. 'She ice. She cold. She water.'

I knew it was no good. Tomorrow Mr Mantolini would cast the ice girl out into the alley.

The next day I wagged school. I hid in the alley and waited. The minutes dragged their feet. The hours seemed to crawl. But then, as I knew he would,

Mr Mantolini emerged with the ice maiden. He dumped her down by the rubbish bins. Her last resting place was to be among the rotting fish heads in an empty alley.

Mr Mantolini disappeared back into the shop. I rushed over to my ice maiden. She was still covered in frost and had sticky, frozen skin.

My plan was to take her to the butcher. I would pay him to keep the ice maiden in his freezer where I could visit her every day. I hadn't asked him yet. But he couldn't say no, could he?

The sun was rising in the sky. I had to hurry.

The ice maiden still stooped. Still reached out. She seemed to know that her time had come. 'Don't worry,' I said. 'I'll save you.'

I don't know what came over me. I did something crazy. I bent down and gently kissed her on the mouth.

4

It was a long kiss. The longest kiss ever in the history of the world. My lips stuck to hers. My flesh froze onto the ice. Cold needles of pain numbed my lips. I tried to pull away but I couldn't. The pain made my eyes water. Tears streamed down my face and across the ice maiden's cheeks.

On we kissed. And on. And on. I wanted to pull my mouth away but much as I cared for the ice girl, I didn't want my lips to tear away, leaving bleeding skin as a painful reminder of my madness. There I was, kissing ice lips, unable to move.

I tried to yell for help but I couldn't speak. Muffled grunts came out of my nose. Horrible nasal noises. No one came to help me. The alley echoed with the noise.

I grabbed the ice maiden and lifted her up. She was heavy. Her body was still sticky with frost. My fingers stuck fast. She was my prisoner. And I was hers.

The sun warmed my back. Tears of agony filled my eyes. If I waited there she would melt. I would be free but the ice maiden would be gone. Her lovely nose and chin would drip away to nothing.

But the cold touch of the ice girl was terrible. Her smiling lips burnt my flesh. The tip of my nose was frozen. I ran out of the alley into the street. There was a group of people waiting by a bus-stop near the end of the pier. 'Help, get me unstuck. But don't hurt the ice maiden,' was what I tried to say.

But what came out was, 'Nmn nnmmm nnnn nng ng ng mn nm.'

The people looked at me as if I was crazy. Some of them laughed. They thought I was acting the fool. An idiot pretending to kiss a statue.

I ran over to Mr Mantolini's shop and tried to knock on the window with my foot. I had to balance on one leg, while holding the ice girl in my arms and painfully kissing her at the same time. I fell over with a crunch. Oh agony, oh misery, oh pain. My lips, my fingers, my knees.

There was no sign of Mr Mantolini. He must have been in the back room.

5

What could I do? I looked out to sea. If I jumped into the water it would melt the ice. My lips and fingers would come free. But the ice maiden would melt. 'Let me go,' I whispered in my mind. But she made no answer.

My hands were numb. Cold pins pricked me without mercy. I ran towards the pier. I spoke to my ice maiden again, without words. 'I'm sorry. I'm sorry, sorry, sorry.'

I jogged along the pier. Further and further. My feet drummed in time with my thoughts. 'Sorry, sorry, sorry.'

I stopped and stared down at the waves. Then I closed my eyes and jumped, still clutching the ice-cold girl to my chest. Down, I plunged. For a frozen moment I hung above the ocean. And then, with a gurgle and a groan, I took the ice lady to her doom.

The waves tossed above us. The warm water parted our lips. My fingers slipped from her side. I bobbed up like an empty bottle and saw her floating away. Already her eyes had gone. Her hair was a glassy mat. The smiling maiden smiled no more. She was just a lump of ice melting in the waves.

'No,' I screamed. My mouth filled with salt water and I sank under the sea.

They say that your past life flashes by you when you are drowning. Well, it's true. I re-lived some horrible moments. I remembered the time in a small country school when I was just a little kid. And the only redhead. I saw the school bully Johnson teasing me every day. Once again I sat on the school bench at lunch time – alone and rejected. Not allowed to hang around with the others. Just because Johnson didn't like red hair. Once again I could hear him calling me 'carrots' and 'ginger'. They were the last thoughts that came to me before the world vanished into salty blackness.

6

But I didn't drown. In a way my hair saved me. It must have been easy for them to spot my curly locks swirling like red seaweed thrown up from the ocean bed.

Mr Mantolini pulled me out. He and his cousin. I could hear him talking even though I was only half conscious. 'You live. But you not die yet.'

I didn't want to open my eyes. I couldn't bear to think about what I had done to the ice maiden. I was alive but she was dead. Gone for ever.

In the end I looked up. I stared at my rescuers. Mr Mantolini and his cousin.

She had red tangled hair. And smiling lips. Her eyes sparkled like frozen diamonds. I tell you this. That girl Tony was something else. She was fantastic.

'You're beautiful,' I said under my breath. 'Beautiful.'

Mr Mantolini's ice statue had been good. But not as good as the real thing. After all, it had only been a copy of his cousin Tony. I smiled up at her. And she smiled back. With a real smile.

I guess that's when I discovered that an ice maiden who is dead is not sad. And a nice maiden who is red is not bad.

Not bad at all.

Birdman

Li Foo walked into the water pushing the little raft in front of him. He wiped a tear from his eye and sadly tied a vase to the mast. Then he pushed the raft out to sea and walked back towards the rocky shore. The raft drifted slowly out into the vast Indian Ocean. Li Foo knew that he would never see it again.

1

Sean flapped his wings nervously. It was a long way down to the beach. Everything was set. The feathers were glued on really well. The wooden struts were strong. But would he fly? 'Go on,' said Spider. 'There's only one way to find out.' Deefa barked loudly and ran around their legs, waiting for the fun.

'It's all right for you,' said Sean. 'You're not going in the competition.' Suddenly he ran towards the edge of the sand dune and jumped. He plunged into mid-air and flapped his arms furiously. Panic filled his face. He flapped harder. 'No,' he yelled. 'No.' He plunged down, rolled over in the sand and lay still.

Spider ran down to meet him. 'Are you okay?' he shouted. Sean lifted up a sandy face and nodded. He undid his wings and left them on the sand.

'It'll never work,' said Spider. 'You'll never win the Birdman Competition like that. You can't jump off the end of a pier in those.'

'It doesn't matter,' said Sean. 'I'm going to pick up Uncle Jeremy's hang-glider this afternoon. A real one. You watch me fly over the waves when I get that. This year Buggins isn't going to win for once.'

The two boys walked along the edge of the water. Neither of them noticed the raft at first.

Sean suddenly did six cartwheels along the beach. 'Beat that,' he said.

'That's nothing,' said Spider. 'Watch this.' He tried to stand on his hands but he collapsed onto his face. He stood up and spat out sand. 'That one didn't count,' he grinned. He tried again and the same thing happened. His whole face was covered in sand. It didn't matter how often he tried, Spider just couldn't do cartwheels. Not to save his life.

'Weak,' said a loud voice.

They both looked up. It was Buggins. Big fat Buggins sitting up there on Devil, his big fat horse. He walked Devil past Sean and Spider and then backed up into them. The horse's legs stumbled and spat up sand. Sean and Spider fell back into the waves.

Buggins stared down at them with a smug smile. Then he nodded towards Sean's wings on the beach. 'You'll never win with those,' he scoffed. 'You just watch me tomorrow. 'I'll take the trophy off again for sure.'

He kicked his horse and galloped along the beach. 'Oh, look,' yelled Sean. 'The dirty ratbag.'

Buggins galloped straight towards Sean's wings. Devil's hoofs pounded into the feathers and plastic. The wings were smashed to pieces.

Sean and Spider stared in dismay. The wings were completely ruined. And to make matters worse, there on top of them was a pile of steaming horse manure. Dropped there by Devil.

Deefa loved horse manure. He barked twice and shoved his face right in it. He pushed his nose into the putrid pile. He rubbed his ears in too. It was a dog's heaven.

Buggins stopped a little way off. He felt safe sitting up there on Devil.

'You wait,' yelled Sean. 'You just wait.' It was a weak thing to say and he knew it. He was so angry that he just couldn't think of anything else. Buggins laughed horribly and galloped away along the beach. With a weary heart Sean watched him disappear.

'Don't worry,' said Spider. 'You've still got your uncle's hang-glider. These wings didn't work anyway.'

Suddenly Sean saw something. 'Look,' he screamed. 'Over there.' He pointed to where the edge of a little raft poked out of the sand.

2

Spider started to scratch away at the sand with his hands. Sean ran over and helped. 'Wow,' said Spider. 'I wonder where this came from.' The raft had been washed in by the tide. After a bit of tugging and digging they finally pulled it out. They stared at the strange vase tied to the mast.

'There could be anything in there,' said Spider. 'Open it up, Sean.'

Sean brushed at the sand on the vase. There was

weird writing on the outside. And a skull and crossbones.

They looked at each other and shrugged. Neither wanted to be the one to open the vase. In the end Sean grabbed the lid and pulled. It came off with a pop. A whiff of grey smoke puffed out. Spider moved back up the beach to safety. Sean looked at his mate. Spider was a good kid but he could be a bit of a wimp at times.

Sean carefully untied the vase and tipped it up. An animal slipped out. A stiff, hard animal like a cat.

They stared at the rigid body. Its eyes were closed. Its fur was matted and wiry. Its legs hung down like open arms.

'Wow,' Sean whistled. 'I've never seen anything like that before.' He turned it upside down. It was hollow in the middle.

'It's a hat,' said Spider. 'A cat hat. Give me a go.' He snatched the cat hat from Sean's arms.

'Don't wreck it,' said Sean. 'It could be valuable.'

Spider put the cat hat on his head. The legs reached down under his chin. It looked as if the cat was hanging onto his face. It seemed weird, perched up there on Spider's hair.

'Give me a shot,' said Sean. Spider shook his head. He was very attached to the hat.

Sean smiled to himself. 'Okay,' he said. 'Suit yourself.' He walked towards the wings and pretended he wasn't interested in the cat hat. He did another five cartwheels – right past Spider.

THE CAT HAT'S EYES CLICKED OPEN.

IT SAW A BOY TURNING

CARTWHEELS ON THE SAND.

THE EYES CLICKED CLOSED AGAIN.

Spider, who was still wearing the cat hat, stared at Sean with a funny sort of look on his face. Then he did five perfect cartwheels on the sand. They were terrific.

'Wow,' Sean yelled. 'Good one, Spider. Fantastic.' Sean really was impressed. Spider could do fantastic cartwheels. And just a minute before he couldn't even stand on his hands.

Spider looked pretty surprised himself. He shook his head wisely. 'You can learn a lot from me, Sean,' he said. He brushed down the cat hat.

'Maybe it brings good luck,' said Sean.

'Yeah,' said Spider. 'Like a lucky rabbit's foot.'

They walked up the track towards home. On the edge of the cliff a fat man was standing looking out to sea. He suddenly opened his mouth and burped loudly.

THE CAT HAT'S EYES CLICKED OPEN.

IT SAW A MAN BURPING.

THE EYES CLICKED CLOSED AGAIN.

Spider suddenly felt ill. As if he had eaten about fifty meat pies for breakfast. He tried to swallow but couldn't. He tried to hold everything down. But it was no use. Spider opened his mouth and let out an enormous burp.

'Beauty,' yelled Sean. 'What a ripper.' He was filled with admiration. Spider was pleased with himself. Usually he couldn't do very good burps at all.

3

That afternoon Spider and Sean went down to the railway station to pick up Uncle Jeremy's hang-glider. Spider still had the cat hat perched on his head.

The bloke in the railway station pretended that the boys weren't there, like railway workers often do. 'Excuse me,' Sean said. 'We've come for a hang-glider.' The bloke didn't take any notice. He just went on reading a magazine. Sean tapped on the window-sill with a coin. The porter looked up savagely.

'Can't you see I'm busy,' he growled in a deep voice. 'Wait your turn.' Sean and Spider looked around. There wasn't another person in sight.

After ages and ages the porter came to the window. 'Where's your receipt?' he asked.

'I lost it,' Sean said. 'But the hang-glider's addressed to Sean Tuttle.'

This is when Sean heard the terrible words. 'It's not here. Sean Tuttle picked it up this morning. He was with two other kids.'

'What,' Sean yelled. 'Which kids?'

'I don't know. Just kids.'

'Buggins,' Sean shouted.

'And Thistle and Wolf,' added Spider. 'They've nicked it.'

'You're responsible,' Sean said to the porter. 'The railways have to get it back. Buggins didn't have a receipt.'

The porter glared at them. 'And neither do you,' he said. 'You kids buzz off and don't tell me how to do my job.' He was starting to get angry.

THE CAT HAT'S EYES CLICKED OPEN.

IT SAW A PORTER TALKING.

THE EYES CLICKED CLOSED AGAIN.

Spider spoke in a deep, man's voice. He sounded

exactly like the porter. A great big booming voice, coming out of a boy's mouth. 'You kids buzz off,' he said. 'And don't tell me how to do my job.'

'Right,' yelled the porter. Man, was he mad. He headed for the door. Spider and Sean turned and ran for it.

'You shouldn't have done that, Spider,' Sean said when they finally stopped running.

'It was this hat,' Spider said. 'It made me do it. And its eyes open. I'm sure I heard its eyes click that time I burped.' He took the cat hat off his head. 'Here, you have it.'

4

When they reached home, Sean's father was looking a bit sheepish. 'Is she talking to you yet?' asked Sean. His father shook his head.

Sean smiled to himself. Poor Dad. He was in big trouble. He had agreed to let Sean fly in the Birdman Competition without telling Mum and she was mad at him. She thought it was too dangerous. Dad tried to kid her and joke about it but she wouldn't even crack a smile.

'Buggins has pinched the hang-glider,' said Sean.

Mr Tuttle didn't hear him. He was peering anxiously out of the window. His wife was heading for the door. He held a finger up to his lips. 'Sh . . .' he said. 'Not a word about it in front of your mother.' He suddenly saw the cat hat. 'What on earth is that?'

'A cat hat,' Sean told him. 'It brings good luck if you put it on your head.'

Mr Tuttle took the cat hat and put it on his own head. 'I can do with a bit of good luck today,' he said with a grin. 'This might cheer Mum up a bit.'

Just then a number of things happened.

The door opened and Mum walked in. She said exactly the same thing. 'What on earth is that?'

Mr Tuttle sure did look stupid with a dead cat perched on his head.

Sean's mum wasn't alone. Deefa had come in after her. A very hungry Deefa. He gave two woofs and trotted over to the food bowl which was still on the floor. It was full of that horrible canned food that dogs love. A sort of wobbling mound of brown jelly. Deefa trotted over and started to gobble away noisily.

THE CAT HAT'S EYES CLICKED OPEN.

IT SAW A DOG EATING A PLATE OF DOG FOOD.

THE EYES CLICKED CLOSED AGAIN.

A strange look came into Mr Tuttle's eyes. He dropped down onto his hands and knees. 'Woof, woof,' he said. He trotted over to the food bowl and started gobbling at the dog food with Deefa. They licked their lips and swallowed the stuff down like crazy.

The kids' eyes nearly popped out of their heads. So did Sean's mum's. No one could believe what they were seeing. Mr Tuttle was eating yucky, cold dog food. From the same bowl as the dog. Deefa growled. Mr Tuttle barked back. They were fighting over the dog food.

Mr Tuttle suddenly stood up with a wild look in his eyes. He didn't know what was going on. He was confused. And his face was smeared with gravy and bits of horrible meat stuff. 'Ruth,' he gasped, 'I didn't mean to do that. It wasn't what . . .' His voice trailed off. He didn't know what to say. Then he grinned.

Mrs Tuttle was trying hard not to smile but she just couldn't stop herself. 'What's for dessert?' she said with a chuckle. The row was over. They were talking again.

Still and all, Sean thought it was better not to mention the stolen hang-glider. He and Spider were on their own.

Sean looked at the hat. He suddenly had an idea but he pushed it out of his mind. His glider was gone. Buggins and his mates had stolen it. Life just wasn't fair sometimes.

5

'We'll have to use our own plane like all the other kids,' Sean said to Spider. They were walking along the cliff, looking for Buggins.

'What about the cat hat?' said Spider. 'It copies things. It opens its eyes and copies what it sees. I know it does.'

'It's dangerous,' Sean told him. 'You never know what it's going to stare at. Look what happened to Dad.'

'We could figure something out,' said Spider. If you wore the cat and it opened its eyes and saw something . . .' His voice was drowned out by a roar. They both looked up as a jumbo jet streaked across the sky.

Before he could think any more about it, Sean saw what he had been looking for. It was Buggins and his mates.

Buggins took a short run along the top of a sand

dune and launched out into the air. He clung on to a wonderful red and blue hang-glider. Sean's hang-glider. Buggins swooped about three metres above the sand and then did a wobbly landing on the beach.

Wolf and Thistle pelted down after him. 'Fantastic,' yelled Thistle.

'We're onto a winner,' said Wolf.

'My winner,' Sean said in a tough voice. 'You stole my hang-glider.'

Buggins looked up. 'Get real,' he sneered. 'I've been saving up for this for months. Ask my dad if you like.'

'Hand it over,' Sean said.

Buggins bunched up his fist. 'Come and get it,' he jeered. He walked towards Sean with heavy steps. His two mates were next to him.

'We're not scared of you,' yelled Spider. 'Flatten him, Sean.'

Buggins took another couple of steps forward. There was only one thing to do. So Sean did it. He turned and ran for his life. Spider pelted after him. How humiliating. Sean could hear Wolf, Thistle and Buggins jeering as he ran.

Sean spent the rest of the day trying to mend his

bird wings. He used brand new materials. Plastic, wood and wire as well as the feathers. After a couple of hours he put down his tools. He didn't think he could finish in time. There was only one more day left and it was a school day.

'That'll never fly,' said Spider. 'The ones the kids make always crash. We need something else. A bit of help.' He held up the cat hat and winked.

6

'No way,' said Sean. 'Not without testing it first anyway.'

Spider looked at the broken wings. 'But they're busted,' he said.

Sean nodded. 'So, we'll try it out on something else.'

The next day Sean took the cat hat to school.

His plan was to muck around down near the oval while the athletes were practising for the school sports.

There was this kid named Innes who was in Year Twelve. He was a champion high jumper. Sean decided to hang around near him with the hat on. The cat hat would open its eyes and see Innes. Sean

26

would immediately do a wonderful high jump in front of all the kids.

Of course Sean didn't know whether or not the silly thing would open its eyes. That was the only weakness with the plan.

As it happened, the cat hat did open its eyes.

Just as a group of girls jogged up in their tracksuits. At that very moment Innes was running up for a jump. Sean slipped the cat hat over his head. He had to be quick. The jump would be over in a flash. Sean quite liked the idea of doing a great leap in front of the girls.

But they didn't even look at him once. They headed into the girls' changing room.

THE CAT HAT'S EYES CLICKED OPEN.

IT SAW GIRLS GOING INTO THE CHANGING ROOM.

THE EYES CLICKED CLOSED AGAIN.

Sean tried to stop his legs going. He hung onto the fence. But it was no good. Some inner force made him go. Made him follow the girls into their changing room. It was as if he was in a trance. He jogged straight in after them.

The next thing Sean knew – there he was. Surrounded by girls – in their changing room. He

27

opened his mouth to cry out in horror but nothing came out. The girls screamed and yelled. They threw shoes. 'Nerd. Weirdo,' screamed a girl called Esmeralda. Talk about terrible.

Spider just shook his head and grinned while the screaming mob of girls chased Sean clear out of the school.

Buggins and Thistle and Wolf saw the whole thing. They thought it was a great joke.

It was the worst moment of Sean's life. He walked home with a heart full of pain. Talk about embarrassing. Before long everyone in the school would know about it. That cat hat was not to be trusted.

7

All that he could do now was fix up his birdman wings so that they would fly. Sean worked nearly all night. He glued and cut and nailed. Until finally the wings were finished. He didn't even have time to try them out. The competition started first thing in the morning. He would just have to jump off the end of the pier and hope for the best.

'You'll never beat Buggins,' said Spider as they

walked towards the pier. 'He's got a proper hang-glider.'

'My hang-glider,' Sean said.

'Use the cat hat,' said Spider. 'We wait until a plane goes over, the cat hat opens its eyes and we're off. Up, up and away.'

'What do you mean, *we're* off. It's me that will be off. Not you. No way. That cat hat is not to be trusted. It stays in my bag out of harm's way.'

And that's how Sean came to be standing there on the end of the pier with his bird wings. With all the others. There were kids everywhere. About two hundred looking on and a mob of competitors.

The planes were fantastic. There were biplanes and triplanes. There were rockets and rickety old things built on top of prams. Mostly they were made out of plastic and wood and paper. Some were like parachutes. Others like helicopters.

None of them had engines. The planes had to glide or be powered by human energy. You could pedal. You could flap. And you could jump. But no other form of power was allowed.

The winner was the one who could get furthest away from the pier.

'Okay, okay, okay, fans,' yelled Wolf. He shouted

at everyone through a megaphone. 'The first entry in this year's Birdman Competition is . . . me.'

A cheer went up. Wolf's plane was in the shape of a giant beer can. His legs stuck out at the bottom. His arms poked out of the side like skinny wings. His head was like a marble on the top. Everyone, including Wolf, knew what was going to happen when he jumped off the end of the pier.

'This model,' he yelled, 'runs on brain power and force of will. It's shaped to have minimum wind resistance.' He waddled over to the side of the pier. And jumped.

It was a very high pier. Wolf flew through the air with the greatest of ease. Like a brick. Straight down. He hit the water with an enormous 'thunk'. The beer can broke up and Wolf swam to the ladder on the side of the pier. Everyone cheered and laughed. Kids patted him on the back. If ever there was a showman it was Wolf.

Next it was the turn of a kid called Egan. He had a slide rigged up on the end of the pier. He sat up on the top inside a huge Batplane. Wolf called for silence. The crowd knew that Egan had a good chance of winning. He was a serious competitor. Wolf climbed up the slide. 'What are the specifications of this aircraft?' he asked.

Egan sat in the cockpit dressed in a black wetsuit. He wore black goggles to match his plane. 'It has a five metre wing-span,' he said. 'The construction is canvas stretched on a wooden frame. At the bottom of the ramp it reaches a speed of fifteen knots – enough to carry me forty metres from the edge of the pier.'

The crowd clapped. Everyone was impressed.

Egan's helpers pushed him off. The Batplane gathered speed. It raced down the slide and launched into the air. It swooped upwards for a second or two. Then it hung in the air and plunged down into the sea. The Bat-pilot swam sadly back to the cheers and claps of a disappointed crowd.

8

'The next competitor,' shouted Wolf, 'is Thistle.' There were cheers, and some boos.

Thistle had a huge triplane made out of clear plastic. The three layers of wings were so wide that everyone had to be moved back. The wings hung over both sides of the pier. Thistle's legs stuck out through the bottom of the fuselage.

Thistle held his arms up in a boxer's victory wave. Then he ran towards the water and hurtled over the edge of the pier.

The wings of the plane broke off in mid-air and Thistle torpedoed down into the water. The wings fluttered down after him.

This is how it went on for ages and ages. Plane after plane plunged over the edge. None of them got very far at all. So far, the Batplane had flown furthest from the pier.

Sean's stomach felt all wobbly inside. 'At least if I win the competition it will make up for me going into the girls' changing room,' he thought to himself. But his heart sank. He knew he couldn't win. He felt terrible. Deefa yapped and ran around his feet.

The competition was almost over. There were only two entries left.

'And now,' announced Wolf, 'we have an entry from that dashing young man – Jack Buggins.' Buggins gave the crowd a mock bow. Then he looked at the girls and smiled. Sean's heart sank when he saw a lot of them smiling back.

Buggins pushed through the crowd and came out holding his hang-glider above his head. Or more correctly, Sean's hang-glider. There was a gasp from the mob. It was a beautiful craft. There was no doubt at all about who was going to win.

Buggins ran to the edge of the pier and launched himself off. A gentle breeze took the hang-glider and lifted it into the air. Buggins sailed and swooped above the water. He circled around and even let go with one hand and waved to the crowd.

Then he sailed out to sea and made a graceful landing about fifty metres away. The crowd went crazy. Buggins had won by a mile. No one had ever gone that far before.

Buggins swam back to the pier with the glider. Everyone patted him on the back. He gave a victory wave and leered at Sean.

'Ladies and gentlemen,' said Wolf. 'There is one more contestant – if you can call him that. The feathered freak, Sean Tuttle.'

Sean was ready. And he felt ridiculous with the two feathered wings strapped onto his arms. He flapped them up and down feebly. Everyone laughed. The whole lot of them. Sean looked like a plucked chook.

In the distance and high above, a crop-dusting plane circled the coast. 'Put this on,' whispered Spider urgently. He reached into a bag and pulled out the cat hat.

Sean shook his head. Spider nodded towards the plane. 'This is your only chance,' he said.

Sean stared at the girls who were hanging around Buggins, looking at the hang-glider in admiration. 'What the heck,' he said to himself. 'It's worth the risk.' He put the cat hat on his head and tottered over to the edge of the pier.

'Tuttle is wearing a new form of life jacket,' said Wolf. 'When he crashes his dead cat swims back with him.' Everyone laughed. Except Sean and Spider.

The crop-dusting plane approached the pier. 'Now,' said Spider. The plane flew into a bank of clouds and disappeared.

THE CAT HAT'S EYES CLICKED OPEN.

IT SAW NOTHING BUT EMPTY SKY.

THE EYES CLICKED CLOSED AGAIN.

Nothing happened. Sean still stood there shivering on the end of the pier. Dressed in his foolish, feathered wings. With the cat hat perched up on his head. The noise of the plane disappeared into the distance.

'Well, come on,' said Wolf. 'Get going.'

'He's scared,' sneered Buggins.

'What a chicken,' said Thistle.

'It opened its eyes,' said Spider. 'But too late. The plane's gone.'

'I'm done for,' said Sean. He looked down into the water. It was a long way. His legs were knocking. He couldn't bring himself to jump. 'Ten seconds,' yelled Wolf. 'Jump or you're disqualified.'

9

Sean took a deep breath and stared along the pier. A seagull sat on a post.

THE CAT HAT'S EYES CLICKED OPEN.
IT SAW A SEAGULL FLAP ITS WINGS
FURIOUSLY AND FLY UP INTO THE SKY.
THE EYES CLICKED CLOSED AGAIN.

Sean's wings started to whir. They flapped so fast that he couldn't see them. He thought his arms were going to fall off. Up he went, buzzing like a fantastic dragonfly.

The water fell far below. At first Sean's head swam. The kids looked like ants on the pier. Birds fluttered around. What if he fell?

But then, for some reason, he knew he was safe. He felt like a bird. He was flying as if he had been born with wings. He looped the loop. He plunged down and skimmed the waves and then soared up again above the crowd. He flew sideways and upside

35

down. He twirled and twisted. He flapped like a feathery fiend.

Everyone gasped. Their mouths fell open. Their eyes bugged out. A sigh swept the pier. Sean plunged down and buzzed just above their heads like a dive-bomber. The kids threw themselves down as he hurtled overhead.

It was wonderful. It was weird. Sean had no control over what happened. He just did everything the gull did.

'Yahoo,' yelled Spider. 'Go, Sean, go.' He was so excited that he nearly fell off the pier.

Finally Sean and the bird settled on the waves. Sean let the wings sink and swam back to the waiting crowd.

10

You should have heard the cheering. And shouting No one had ever seen anything like it before. One of the girls gave him a little peck on the cheek.

Buggins was as mad as a snake. He pushed to the front.

'Tuttle cheated,' he yelled. 'That cat thing did it. It was a powered flight.'

Buggins pulled the cat hat off Sean's head. And put it on his own. 'It's alive,' he said. 'It opened its eyes. I saw it.' Buggins looked kind of pathetic with the cat hat perched on his skull.

He peered along the pier to where Devil was tied up. He saw Sean's dog trotting along towards the horse.

THE CAT HAT'S EYES CLICKED OPEN.

IT SAW A DOG RUNNING TOWARDS THE HORSE.

IT SAW HIM PUSHING HIS HEAD INTO A PILE OF HORSE MANURE.

THE EYES CLICKED CLOSED AGAIN.

Buggins felt his legs starting to carry him along the pier. 'No,' he screamed. 'No, no, no.'

But nothing . . .

        could stop him . . .

                rushing towards the manure.

Little Squirt

Inside the toilet five boys are peeing in the air to see how high they can get. They are having a competition before the athletics start. My big brother Sam is winning as usual. No one can pee as high as he can. I go red in the face when I see them. 'Come on, Weesle,' he says to me. 'Have a go.'

I don't want to have a go really. It is embarrassing and I am not very good at it. He is asking me on purpose. He wants me to make a fool of myself again. 'Yeah,' say all the others. 'Come on, Weesle. Don't be a wimp.'

Oh, it is awful. They are all jeering at me. I will have to be in it. I undo my fly and have a try. I am so nervous that only a little dribble comes out. They all laugh and mock. 'Weak,' they yell. My brother Sam is the worst of the lot. 'Poor Weesle is a little squirt,' he says. They all crack up and laugh like mad.

We go out to athletics practice. I am in the hundred metres and so is Sam. Next week it will be the big run-off to see who is the fastest boy in the school. Today is just a try-out. How I wish I could win. I would do anything to beat my brother Sam.

But my heart is heavy inside me. He is better than me at everything. He is smarter than me. He is better-looking than me. He is taller than me. He is tougher than me. He can beat me at anything you care to name.

We crouch down at the starting line. 'I'll wait for you at the end, wimp,' jeers Sam. 'That is if you get there at all.'

The other boys are looking on. Oh, how I would love to beat Sam. I don't even care if I am not the winner. Just so long as I beat Sam. He is always showing off. He is always making me feel like a wimp.

Mr Hendrix has the starter's gun in his hand. My knees are starting to wobble I am so nervous. And this is not even the real race when the whole school will be watching. This is just a practice.

'Bang.' We are off. I get away to a good start. I am ahead by a couple of metres. Suddenly everything seems to go right. My legs whirr. I romp along easily. My breathing is steady. I look behind and Sam seems to be in trouble. I am in front and he is second. I am nearly up to the finishing line. For the first time in my life I am going to beat him at something.

I grin as I approach the string. But I grin too soon. Sam flashes by me so quickly that I can't believe it. He has beaten me again. I feel terrible. I try not to let tears show in my eyes.

Sam is jumping around and showing off. He holds his hands over his head like a boxer. 'I hung back on purpose,' he jeers. 'Thought you had me, didn't you, wimp?' he says. He gloats and shows off all the way home.

The other boys join in and tease me too.

I walk sadly along behind them. I try not to listen. Next Tuesday is the real race. I will never be able to beat Sam in that. I will be too nervous. I am just not good enough.

Sam goes off with the others to explore the big forest. They won't let me go with them. 'You'd only get lost,' says Sam.

2

Tears are in my eyes as I reach home. I try to dry them before Mum notices but once again I fail.

'What's the matter, Weesle?' says Mum.

'It's Sam,' I yell. 'He always wins at everything. Every time he beats me. He can even tie his shoelaces faster than me. I would love to beat him at something – just once. Today it was running. He won the hundred metres again. He always wins. Next Tuesday is the grand final.'

Mum bends down and puts her arm around me. 'Listen, Weesle,' she says. 'There is one way you can win at anything. I used to be a champion runner and I know.'

This is the first time that I hear about Mum being a champion runner. I look at her, waiting to learn the secret.

'You train,' she says. 'You practise. Every minute. Every day. Sam never trains. He is lazy. If you train every day you can beat him. He just wins because he is bigger than you.'

Mum could be right. I decide to give it a go.

I get up early in the morning and I train. I train at recess. I train at lunch-time. I train after school. I train in the hot weather and I train when it is cold. I get better and better, especially on the cold days. It is hard work. It is not easy. But I am determined to beat Sam. No one has ever trained as hard as I do.

Mum would be proud of me if she could see how hard I train. But I do it in secret. I am going to surprise Sam. No one is going to expect me to win. I can't wait to see the look on his face.

Tuesday comes at last. This is it. This is my big chance. All my training is going to pay off. It is cold so I wear my thick jumper to school.

I walk into the toilet where Sam and the boys are having the grand final. They are seeing which boy in the school will be the Grand Champion at peeing in the air. 'Give me a go,' I say. They laugh and jeer and call me squirt. But I don't care. I have been training for this all week.

Boy, do I squirt. I pee higher than anyone in the world has ever done. Higher than my head. The kids' eyes bug out with admiration. 'Wow,' they yell.

Sam, however, does not admire me. He is as mad as a hatter. He blows his top. He hits the roof.

But not in the same way that I do.

The Mouth Organ

I am not happy standing here in front of the magnolia tree. I play my guitar and peer at my hat on the ground. There's not much money in it. Not much at all. There are only about fifty people in this town and they don't have any spare cash. Still, the buses might be good for a dollar. The tourists have plenty of money. They might throw a cent or two to a poor girl. Until they find out that the tree is dead.

My fingers strum the guitar and I sing a sad song. It's called 'The Ballad of Mrs Hardbristle'.

Now here's something. A young bloke crosses the street. He comes over to listen. He has a ponytail and a headband. He doesn't look like he's worth much. He probably hasn't got twenty cents to his name. Still, I keep on playing. Just in case. He puts his hand in his pocket. Maybe he has a twenty-dollar note for me.

The young bloke pulls out his hand. In it he holds a mouth organ. My heart grows heavy. No money. Not a cent. Just a mouth organ. I stop playing and sit down under the tree with a sigh.

Young Ponytail regards me with a grin. 'I know the story,' he says. 'I know what you did.'

How does he know? I've never told anybody. I hang my head with shame and my mind goes back seven years.

2

Mrs Hardbristle sniffed. 'We have to get out of here,' she said. 'Fast.'

I was only six at the time but I will never forget it. I was with Mrs Hardbristle and her little Brownie pack. She looked at us all and then at her husband. 'Mr Hardbristle,' she said. 'There is a bushfire. We have to get back to town.'

Mr Hardbristle had come along to 'look after us', but that was a bit of a joke really. He was all bent over and weak and could hardly keep up with us. He was much older than Mrs Hardbristle.

Some of the girls started to cry as wisps of smoke drifted through the dry bush. Even though we were young, we could imagine the cruel flames and blinding smoke that would soon engulf the very spot where we were standing.

We set off as fast as we could. 'Leave me,' yelled Mr Hardbristle. 'Get the girls to safety.' He puffed and wheezed as he followed along behind.

'Nonsense,' said his wife. She put one of his arms over her shoulder and dragged him behind her like a sack. She was strong, was Mrs Hardbristle. A strong woman.

Twigs crackled under our feet. The hot sun scorched our backs. A kangaroo bounded away in fright, desperately trying to escape the flames. Before long the air was filled with smoke. We started to cough and cry. 'Keep going, girls,' ordered Mrs Hardbristle between gasps. 'Keep going.' She was starting to tire. It was too much really, dragging the old man along behind her.

'Don't stop, Brownies,' she shouted.

And we didn't. Somehow or other we all stumbled through the forest until we reached town. I say town, but it only had six shops and a pub and about twenty houses. I was hoping to see my father there waiting with the car. But there was no one. The dusty street was empty. Not a car. Not a person.

Mrs Hardbristle gently put her husband down in the shade. 'The fire is going to take out the town,' she said. 'Girls, into the middle of the square.'

There was a little grassy patch in the middle of the street with a picnic table there. She ran into the general store and came back with a spade and a large blanket. Without a word she started to dig. Mr Hardbristle tried to help but he was too weak.

Smoke swirled in the air. We could hear the flames now. Crackling in the surrounding forest. The sun was blotted out by smoke. The Brownies' faces were black except for the little rivers made by their tears.

On dug Mrs Hardbristle. On and on and on. The hole became deeper. Sweat poured down her forehead. Her uniform was filthy with dry soil and smoke. The heat was terrible. Suddenly the fire was upon us. The general store exploded like a bomb. Flames ate into the walls.

Mrs Hardbristle stopped digging. 'Get in,' she said. She helped her husband into the hole and I climbed in with the other three Brownies. We felt the blanket placed over our heads. Everything went dark. Suddenly we were wet. She was pouring water over the blanket.

Poor old Mr Hardbristle was worried about his

wife. 'Get in, get in,' he croaked at her.

'I'll be all right,' we heard Mrs Hardbristle say. 'You look after the girls.'

We felt the fire roar past. Its heat stifled us. Its smoke choked us. But its flames did not claim us. We survived.

When we climbed out the town had gone. Not a building was left. Smoke drifted slowly up from charred timber and twisted tin. Just by the hole we found Mrs Hardbristle. Stretched out. Not burnt but suffocated by the smoke. She had saved us all. And had lost her own life. Mr Hardbristle knelt over the still body of his wife and let the silent tears melt into his beard. His shoulders shook in wordless grief.

Mrs Hardbristle was a heroine. She had saved us from the flames and given up her own life. Our parents were so grateful. They said that they would never forget her.

The town was rebuilt. And in the hole where we had sheltered, our parents planted a little magnolia tree in memory of that brave woman.

Mr Hardbristle was filled with despair and guilt. 'I hid in the hole,' he said. 'And let my wife die. I'm a coward.'

Of course he wasn't a coward. He was bent and weak. And anyway, there's nothing to say that the man has to be the brave one. Why shouldn't it be a woman?

But he wouldn't listen. No matter what we said. He wouldn't leave the little cottage that the people built for him. He just sat there on the porch in his old rocking chair staring at the magnolia tree.

I was only a little girl but I told him something that I heard my mother say to Dad. 'There's no need to feel bad. She would want you to be happy.'

He rocked for a long time and then he said, 'When that magnolia tree flowers, then I will know that she has forgiven me. Then I will be happy. But not until then.'

I ran home and told Mum what he said. Mum smiled sadly. 'Magnolia trees sometimes don't flower for seven years,' she said. 'I don't think Mr Hardbristle has seven years left.'

But she was wrong. Seven years passed. And although the magnolia tree didn't flower, Mr Hardbristle still sat there, watching and waiting. It was a fine tree. Tall, with strong, thin branches.

I was thirteen now. And in the Guides. I wanted that tree to flower more than anything. I wanted Mr

Hardbristle to feel forgiven. To know that his wife was smiling upon him.

That's why, in the middle of another hot summer, I decided to water the tree. Our bucket was too small so I filled a big plastic container with water. It once had some sort of powder in it. 'Fertiliser,' I said to myself.

I grasped the wire handle and lugged the water over to the magnolia tree. White powder swirled around in the water. I carefully tipped it out around the roots. Mr Hardbristle sat rocking and watching without saying a word.

In the morning the magnolia tree was dead. Its leaves hung limply, pointing to the ground beneath.

'I can't believe it.' said Dad. He picked up a tiny smudge of white powder on his finger. 'Somebody's poisoned it. They've put blackberry killer on the magnolia.'

I felt like sinking into the ground. I thought it was fertiliser in the bucket. I had killed the tree. I stared over at Mr Hardbristle. His seat was empty. He was in bed and he wouldn't get out. And he would never see the magnolia bloom.

Now there were two guilty people. Mr Hardbristle and me.

No one knew what I had done, except Mr

Hardbristle. I just couldn't own up to it. It was too horrible. I felt like going to bed and staying there myself. I could put my head under the blanket and never come out like he was doing.

But I didn't. I decided to make up for what I had done. I decided to raise money and buy another magnolia tree. A full-grown one. I could even get one that was flowering. Then Mr Hardbristle would feel good again. 'A thousand dollars,' said Mum. 'That's what a full-grown one in a tub would cost. But it wouldn't be the same really, would it?'

I couldn't believe it. A thousand dollars just for a tree. I had no money at all. Not a cent. I picked up my guitar and went down to the magnolia tree. I put my hat on the ground and started to play.

3

Young Ponytail is looking at me with a sort of a smile. He hands over his battered old mouth organ. 'This might help,' he says.

I look at the worn mouth organ and shrug my shoulders. 'I can't play that,' I say. 'Only guitars.' I pat the guitar that my father gave me. Nothing will make me part with it.

The young man puts the mouth organ to his lips and starts to play. Oh, that music. It is beautiful. At times it swells and falls. Then it changes and seems to flitter round inside my head like a flock of bell-birds calling. It is the sound of soft mountain streams. It is the call of the whispering gums. It is the taste of honey on fresh bread. I have never heard music like it. My eyes brim with tears. A burst of sunshine breaks through the clouds.

I take the mouth organ from his outstretched hand. 'Play your own tune,' he says. 'Not other people's. You've got your own melodies, use them.' His smile seems to look into my soul. 'I'll be back for it tomorrow,' he says. 'At twelve o'clock.'

'There's school tomorrow,' I say. 'Meet me at the front gate. I'll be there. Don't worry about that.'

'Make sure you are,' he says. 'Make sure you are. I have to be movin' on.'

I lean my guitar against the tree and watch him disappear down the street towards the river. I guess he is camping out there.

The mouth organ is chipped and worn. It has played many melodies from long-forgotten lives. I can see that. I am just about to hold it to my lips when a tourist bus pulls up.

Ever since the magnolia tree was planted tourists have been coming to look at it. They stop on their way to Sydney. The story of Mr Hardbristle sitting there waiting for the tree to bloom was in the papers. Everyone hopes that they will be there when the tree blooms.

The tourists jump off the bus. A whole mob of them wearing sun-glasses and shorts. They have cameras around their necks. They want to take a photo of the tree. They bustle up and fall silent.

'It's dead,' says the bus driver as he stares at the tree. They all look at the limp leaves. They turn around and start to climb back onto the bus. I will never earn any money this way. I put the mouth organ to my lips and try to think of a tune. 'Hang down your head, Tom Dooley. Hang down your head and cry'. It is the only tune I can think of. I start to play it. Mournful, sad notes.

The tourists start to sniff. An American in a big hat takes out his handkerchief and blows his nose. A Japanese lady bursts into tears. The tune is so sad. This mouth organ seems to have a strange power. Soon all the tourists are crying. They are leaning on each other's shoulders and weeping. They are not putting any money into my hat.

Something has gone wrong. The mouth organ is not having the right result. I try to think of a happy song. Something comes into my mind. The cancan. I play a bright, happy dance. The tourists link arms. They start to kick their legs up into the air, first one way and then the other. On they go. On and on. They can't throw money into my hat with their arms linked together. I reach the end of the tune and stop. So do they.

They look at each other with wide open eyes. They don't know what is going on. They rush for the bus. They are leaving without donating anything towards the new magnolia tree. I look over the road at Mr Hardbristle's empty rocking chair. I have to do something quick.

I play another tune. 'Kookaburra sits on the old gum tree'. It is bright and happy. The tourists are bright and happy as they scramble up the re-grown gum trees along the street. They sit on the branches like birds. I try to stop playing but I can't. Once you start a tune you seem to have to keep going until you reach the end.

I get up to the bit that goes 'Laugh kookaburra, laugh kookaburra'. They laugh all right – but not the kookaburras. The tourists sit there in the branches with their heads turned up, laughing like jackasses.

Finally I stop. The tourists start to shriek. They are really scared by all this. They scramble down from their perches and head for the bus again. Still they have not given me one cent. I have a last desperate try.

I start to play 'You can leave your hat on' – a real wild tune. The tourists stop. They start to dance. A sliding, writhing dance. The Japanese man undoes his buttons slowly. He throws his jacket to the ground. The American is flicking off his shoes. Three others are pulling off their jumpers in slow, rhythmic movements. A fat lady is rolling down her stockings. Oh no. I have chosen striptease music.

I try to stop playing but I can't. I have to finish the whole tune. Finally it is over. Thirty tourists stand looking at each other. They have nothing on but their underwear. They scream, they shout, they scramble onto the bus. I decide to let them go. This is not working out at all. The bus takes off down the road in a cloud of dust.

4

What happened? This mouth organ is not solving my problem. I will never get another tree for Mr

Hardbristle this way. Then I remember Young Ponytail's words. 'Play your own tune,' he said. 'Not other people's. You've got your own melodies, use them.'

I have never made up a proper tune in my life. What did he mean? I just decide to play about how I feel in my head. I walk over to the shops, throw my hat on the ground and start to blow. From somewhere deep inside me comes the saddest tune. I have never played like this before. I invent it as I go.

The tune is made up of Mr Hardbristle's sorrow. And the tree that I killed. It is mixed with my tears. It is the unspoken story of a girl who made a mistake and a tree that died. The music is so pure that lovers would embrace for ever if they heard it.

Mr Windfall comes out of his new general store. He walks like he is in a dream. He stands and watches without moving. His eyes are glass – they see things that no one knows. I stop playing for a moment. 'Don't stop,' he pleads. 'Don't stop.' He takes out twenty dollars from his wallet and throws it into my hat. I smile and play on.

Others gather. They crowd around. There is Mr Ralph, our teacher. He wears a smile that is as soft as the clouds. Sue Rickets and two other tough kids from Year Seven stop and listen. Sue Rickets hates my guts. But not now. The music has mellowed her. I look around at the people. They are all on a journey. A special journey. The music takes them where usually they cannot go.

In the end I stop playing. I am out of breath. The crowd stands for a bit without moving. Then they suddenly shake themselves. Mr Ralph reminds me of an old dog coming out of a dream. Everyone puts money in the hat. Then they float away on the wings of their memories. I look into my hat. I have taken eighty-four dollars.

If this keeps up I will earn the thousand dollars for a new tree in no time. No time at all. I look at my watch. I have to get home and chop some wood before tea. I run for it.

Tea is over. The dishes are washed. I sit in front of the fire. Mum and Dad like me to play my guitar when the fire is flickering.

But I do not play the guitar. I take out the mouth organ. The tunes I play on the mouth organ have no names. Nor words. Just melodies that speak to the heart. I play a tune about Grandma. It is a jumpy, happy tune. She is tickling me like she used to.

I laugh and squirm in my mind as I play. It is almost real. All the pain of loss is gone. There is only happiness.

I look at Mum. Her smile is filled with love. I know that, in her mind, Grandma is holding her in her arms like when she was a baby. In the end we all fall asleep. Me and Mum and Dad. There in front of the fire.

It is morning already. Mum is happier than I have ever seen her. My mouth organ has given her joy. I can't part with this mouth organ. I wonder if Young Ponytail will swap it for my guitar. But I can't part with that either. Dad would never forgive me. He gave it to me for Christmas.

I take the eighty-four dollars and wedge it inside my guitar. I put my mouth organ in a deep pocket. Then I head off for school.

This mouth organ can earn me the thousand dollars for a new tree. But can it do it before twelve o'clock?

5

Our school has only one teacher. And twenty kids. We all learn together in the same room. The big kids help the little kids. Mr Ralph helps everyone.

He is a quiet teacher. He never shouts. Everybody likes him.

Mr Ralph looks at me. 'Nicole has hidden talents,' he says. 'She can play the mouth organ.' The kids all look up.

'Play for us,' says Mr Ralph.

I pick up my mouth organ and start to blow. Whatever I think of comes out in the music. The kids all put their heads on the desks. They see what I see. They dream my dreams. The music does it all.

I take them sailing on sparkling oceans. I fly them through the clouds. I show them the bottom of the sea and the highest mountain peaks. Places where the air is so crisp it tinkles when you breathe. I shower them in a waterfall. I dust them with moon powder. I rock them in the arms of loved ones long passed on.

All this I do with my mouth organ. The time blows by as unnoticed as the breeze which comes from the river. Soon it is twelve o'clock. The bell rings. It is lunch time.

The mouth organ trembles in my hand. It wants to return to its owner.

But I only have a mere eighty-four dollars. And I need a thousand. The new magnolia tree has to be seven years old. And they are expensive. I will never be happy until I can look Mr Hardbristle in the eye and see that he is smiling.

I run out of the schoolyard. I hide in the pine plantation nearby.

Young Ponytail arrives at the school gate. I see him from my far-off perch in the branches. I see him looking for me. I see him turn and walk sadly towards the river.

I stay up here in the tree until the bell rings. I feel a bit bad for keeping the mouth organ but it is for a good cause. I am going to use it to get another magnolia tree. Then I will give it back. Maybe.

But something is different. Since I decided to keep the mouth organ things have changed. In class no one looks at me. Mr Ralph doesn't ask me to play any more.

I decide to give it a go without being asked. I pick up my mouth organ to play it. My mouth organ? It is not my mouth organ. It feels cold in my hand. Hostile. It doesn't want to play my tune. A little shiver runs up my spine. I grab the mouth organ in trembling fingers and force it up to my lips. I blow strongly. A horrible, blurting sound explodes into the room.

Everyone in the class groans. The noise hurts their ears. I try again and the mouth organ goes crazy in my hands. It twists and turns as if it is alive. It is trying to get away. I grab it even more tightly and try to blow.

Then it happens. Something terrible. I don't know how. I don't know why. But the mouth organ is inside my mouth. It is stuck in sideways, as if I have a banana jammed in there. My cheeks are stretched out on either side. It hurts something awful. The pain is terrible. My eyes water. The mouth organ is a mouth organ indeed.

I stand up and stagger to my feet. As I breathe, the mouth organ screeches in time. In. Out. In. Out. Horrible bellows. I gasp and the mouth organ gasps with me. A terrible tune. The kids clap their hands over their ears. They try to block out the screeching music. Wheezing discords fill the air.

Looks of pain and fear are thrown at me as I stagger towards the door. I am angry. It's not my fault. I am only trying to make up for killing the tree. I am only trying to get money for a new one. Why does everyone hate me now? I hate them back.

The tune is a tune of pain. My music calls up sights from the bottom of dark places. It is the sound of broken hearts, of wars and disease. Of murder and theft. Of revenge and unforgiven accidents. I see all this in the eyes of Mr Ralph and the class. I have stirred up demons from deep within myself.

They come for me. The class close around me with outstretched fingers. Their nails are like claws. I break through and run. I burst out of the door, clutching my guitar in my hands.

6

The sun has gone. A chill wind tears at my streaming eyes. Cold rain begins to fall. The mouth organ screams with each panting breath. I stumble out of the schoolyard. Mr Ralph and the class follow despite the bellowing shrieks from my mouth. They are after my blood. I have turned them into wild animals. My heart thumps against my ribs. My lungs are screaming for rest. The mouth organ plays the tune of my flight for all to hear.

I stagger through the town. The mouth organ is still lodged inside my mouth. I can't get it out. Shopkeepers and farmers join the chase. My tune of tears irritates everyone. They will do anything to stop it. I stumble and fall at the foot of the magnolia tree. I am exhausted. My breath comes in shrieking howls. The crowd surrounds me.

I hate them. Why have they done this to me? Why won't they leave me in peace? I look at the dead tree. I wish they were like it. Made of wood. With wooden hearts.

The mouth organ pumps out my terrible tune of hate with each breath. The crowd suddenly freezes – the kids, the shopkeepers, the farmers, Mr Ralph. Every one of them make my wish come true. They turn to wood in front of my eyes. Wooden faces. Wooden clothes. Wooden hair. Eyes that do not see. I am standing alone. In a street of statues. They no longer thirst for my blood. They stand there like tombstones in the rain. Still. Silent. With raging faces.

For a moment I am numb. I try to pull the mouth organ from my trembling lips but it won't budge. It won't leave its chosen home.

A door bangs open in the street. It is Dr Jenson. He stands for a moment – stunned. Staring at the stiff figures in the street. He is up-wind. He has not heard my tune of terror. He can save me. He is a doctor. He can get this wretched instrument out of my mouth. He runs towards me and then, mid-step, stops. And turns to wood as the first notes reach his ears.

In the silence of the street I suddenly realise what has happened. I can't go home. Mum and Dad will turn to wood too. I can't go anywhere near anyone. There is not a soul who can help me.

Or is there?

7

I wonder if the young man is still down by the river. He is my only hope. It is his mouth organ. If only I can give it back.

I stumble out of town. Past the school. Past Mr Hardbristle's empty porch. Out into the bush. Towards the river. There is no sign of the young man. The cold water of the river flows by uncaring. I follow the bank. Hoping desperately to see the owner of the mouth organ.

In my cheeks I have a mouth organ. And in my hand a guitar.

My feet take me up. And up. The river is far below. I am on a rocky outcrop looking at the chill water lying like dead rope in the valley.

I see him. There he is. His back is towards me.

He is heading into the forest. I scream but no scream comes. Just terrible discords bellowing with every breath.

Fear grabs my heart. What if my music turns the young man to wood? Who will help me then? I try not to breathe. I wave my guitar but his back is towards me. Oh, oh, oh. Who will help me? I wave again. But it is no use signalling to the back of a head.

I search around for a stone. A rock. A branch. Anything to throw down and attract his attention. But there is nothing. The rocky cliff face has been swept clean by the wind. A few leaves wedged in crevices are all I can find. I desperately throw them over the edge but the cruel wind steals every one.

The guitar. It's all I have. I throw it high into the air.

My eighty-four dollars fall out and spin towards the water. The money is gone. And the guitar is tumbling down. The wind seems to take it in soft hands. I think I can hear quiet chords plucked by unseen fingers. The guitar spins and twists and plunges onto an outcrop of rocks near the young man. It splinters into a thousand fragments.

The young man looks up. He sees me and smiles. He waits.

8

It takes me an hour to reach him. An hour. And bloody knees and scratched fingers. An hour of painful tunes, gasped out through the false smile of my stretched lips.

At last I reach him. The sounds of my breath have no effect. He does not turn to wood. He puts his hands to my cheeks and then gently plucks the mouth organ from my mouth.

'It does good for those who do good. And bad for those who do bad,' he says.

Tears run down my cheeks. 'I only wanted to get money for a tree,' I cry. 'But everything went wrong.' I remember the silent statues in the town.

The young man hands me the mouth organ. We both know what has to be done. Without speaking we walk back together.

The people are all standing there. Every one. Still silent. Still made of wood.

I lift the mouth organ to my lips and start to play. It is the sweetest tune. It is the sound of the birth of the world. It is a flower opening. It is a mother's tear plopping on her baby's cheek. It is a foal's first steps. It is the promise of new life.

My wish comes true. Stiff limbs soften. Wooden lips smile. The people are people again. They are caught up by the tune. They are happy. They remember nothing of my hateful melodies. They sway in time to my new tune. All is forgotten.

I look at Mr Hardbristle's window. I can see his face looking out. It disappears. He comes out and stares up at the magnolia tree. The withered leaves are not withered any more. They are green and fresh. My music has brought the magnolia tree back to life.

The young man turns to me and smiles. 'You have one more tune to play,' he says.

I close my eyes and hold the mouth organ to my lips. I just play a tune of love. Nothing more.

When I open my eyes Mr Hardbristle is smiling. Everyone is smiling.

And the magnolia tree is in full bloom.

The Velvet Throne

Mr Simpkin decided to run away from home. But not for twelve hours. When it was dark he would sneak out of bed and tiptoe down the stairs. Gobble wouldn't know. He would be asleep by then. Snoring as usual.

The kettle began to whistle. Mr Simpkin hurried into the kitchen to make Gobble's coffee. Just the way he liked it. Four spoonfuls of sugar. Cream, not milk. Stirred five and a half times. No more, no less. The toaster suddenly popped. Mr Simpkin snatched the toast and buttered it. He had to hurry. Gobble hated cold toast. He was fussy about his food.

The boiled eggs were ready too. All nine of them. Each egg had a little woollen hat to keep it warm.

'Hurry up, idiot,' Gobble called from his bedroom. He was awake. He didn't like to wait for his breakfast.

Mr Simpkin's hands shook. He hurried into his

brother's bedroom. 'Here it is,' he said nervously. 'Everything's just right.'

Gobble tried to sit up in bed. He was very, very fat. The bed sagged. It groaned and creaked. 'Help me up,' ordered Gobble. 'Don't just stand there like a fool.'

Mr Simpkin put the tray on the floor. Then he tried to heave Gobble up onto his pillows. But he couldn't. His arms were too thin. His muscles were too small. He went red in the face as he heaved and strained at the bulging body. Gobble pushed him away. 'Useless. Absolutely useless,' he grunted as he pulled himself up.

With shaking hands Mr Simpkin put the tray on the bed. 'Twelve pieces of toast with jam,' he said. 'And four pieces with orange marmalade. Your favourite.' Mr Simpkin smiled at his fat brother. But the smile soon fell from his face.

'Idiot,' yelled Gobble. 'I ordered twelve pieces with orange marmalade and four with jam.' He picked up a slice of toast and threw it at the wall. For a moment it stuck there, glued to the wallpaper. Then it slid slowly down, leaving a jammy trail behind it.

'Clean that up,' shouted Gobble. 'And then bring me the newspaper. You always forget the paper.'

Mr Simpkin scurried off to fetch a sponge. 'Yes, Arnold,' he whispered.

Gobble's name wasn't really Gobble. It was Arnold. But Mr Simpkin always called him Gobble in his mind. He was too scared to say it out loud. But it made him feel better. He smiled to himself. Arnold would be furious if he knew.

2

Mr Simpkin opened the door of the flat and walked down the stairs to fetch the paper. There were fifteen flights of stairs. He ran as quickly as he could to fetch the paper. He still had to make his own breakfast and then rush off to work. He didn't want to be late.

While Gobble read the paper in bed, Mr Simpkin prepared his own breakfast. He wasn't allowed to eat the eggs. Or the bread. Or the cereals. He took out a can of sheep's eyes and opened it. Last week, while shopping, he had bought a tin of sheep's eyes by mistake – he thought they were oysters. Gobble was furious. 'You bought them,' Gobble shouted. 'So you eat them.'

Mr Simpkin opened the can and shook the

contents onto a plate. The horrible, wobbling eyes slid out with a slurp. They seemed to be staring up at him. The smell was terrible. Mr Simpkin was hungry. But not that hungry. He just couldn't eat them. He put the plate in the fridge and walked towards the door.

'Goodbye, Gobb . . . I mean Arnold,' he called.

'It's pay-day today,' yelled Gobble. 'Make sure you come straight home with the money. And don't open the packet. I don't want you wasting our wages on rubbish.'

'No, Arnold,' whispered Mr Simpkin. He crept off to work. Gobble had never had a job. He just lay in bed eating chocolates and watching television while poor little Mr Simpkin slaved away at the fertiliser factory all day.

At the end of every week Mr Simpkin handed his pay packet over to Gobble. If Gobble was in a good mood he would sometimes give Mr Simpkin a few dollars for himself.

Mr Simpkin just made it to work in time. He spent all day filling up fertiliser bags. It was hard work. He grew hungrier and hungrier. His stomach rumbled. At lunch time he had nothing to eat. Gobble wouldn't let him have any money to buy food until he'd eaten the can of sheep's eyes. He was too scared to tip them down the drain in case Gobble caught him.

'Aren't you having any lunch?' asked Tom Richards, the foreman.

'I'm not hungry,' said Mr Simpkin. He wet his lips and watched sadly as Tom scoffed down his sandwiches.

After work Mr Simpkin collected his pay packet and walked slowly home. Gobble would stuff the money in his pocket. He would tell Mr Simpkin to eat the sheep's eyes for tea. He would fill his face with jellies and cakes while Mr Simpkin watched.

The rain drizzled down. Mr Simpkin walked more and more slowly. He thought about his plans to run away. Why wait until tonight? Why not run off now? Keep the money. It was his money. He could start a new life. Get another job where Gobble couldn't find him.

He could go to a motel for the night.

Gobble had thousands of dollars in a tin under the bed. It was all money that Mr Simpkin had earned. He wished that he could get some of it but he knew that Gobble wouldn't hand it over.

3

The streets were full of people rushing home. It was cold. But Mr Simpkin smiled to himself. He tore open his pay packet. The dollar bills were folded neatly. They were all his. Every one. It made him feel terrific to open his own pay packet.

He would do it. He decided straight away. He would go to a motel and book in. He would order an enormous meal. Gobble could eat the sheep's eyes if he wanted. The thought of it made Mr Simpkin chuckle. A motel. That's where he would go. But first he needed to find a toilet. All of the excitement was making him nervous. He needed to go to the loo.

Nearby was a park. Mr Simpkin ran across the wet grass. Soon he was surrounded by trees. It was growing dark. Where was the toilet? There was one around here somewhere.

There it was. Under the trees. A bluestone building. Like a jail.

Mr Simpkin looked at his watch. Two minutes to five.

He found the MEN sign and hurried inside.

Someone had written on the wall. There was

scribble everywhere. Mr Simpkin didn't read it. Graffiti usually said rude things. He tried not to look at the scrawled writing. But he couldn't help himself. Just above his head was scribbled:

1. *THIS JOINT GETS LOCKED AT FIVE.*

There was a loud clang and the sound of a key turning.

At first Mr Simpkin did nothing. Then he realised. Someone had shut the gate and locked it. He rushed over to the iron gate. It was fixed with a chain and padlock. 'Hey,' he called out softly. 'I'm in here.'

He was too embarrassed to shout. He heard footsteps disappearing. 'Excuse me,' he called softly. 'Er, excuse me.'

The footsteps disappeared. No one answered his call. He was alone. Locked in a public toilet. On a cold and wet night.

He plucked up his courage. 'Help,' he shouted. 'Help, help, help.'

The park was silent. The toilet was silent. He looked up at the roof where one lonely light globe glowed in the dark. There was no way out. He was trapped.

4

The night grew colder. Mr Simpkin shivered and drew his coat around himself. 'Help,' he yelled again. 'Help, help, help.'

The rain dripped silently. There was no answer. He knew no one would come until morning. He looked around for somewhere to sit. The floor was wet and cold. And he was hungry.

He started to look at the graffiti. There was another bit with a number. It said:

2. THE BEST SEAT IN THE HOUSE.

An arrow pointed to one of the cubicles. Mr Simpkin gave a weak grin. Someone had a sense of humour. He followed the arrow into the cubicle. And gasped. The toilet seat was covered in velvet. The pan shone like gold. The cistern button was a diamond. The toilet was more like a throne than a loo.

This was crazy. Why would anyone put such a wonderful seat there? Vandals could wreck it in no time at all.

He stared around the cubicle. There was another piece of numbered graffiti. It read:

3. NO STANDING.

Suddenly Mr Simpkin felt an urgent need to sit down. His legs seemed to make him walk. He shuffled forward and sat on the velvet-lined toilet seat. He tried to stop, but he couldn't. Well, he thought that he couldn't. Maybe he had been feeling a little tired. Yes, that was it.

Something scuffled in the gloom. He stared at the corner. A shadow moved. And scuttered. Mr Simpkin's heart froze. Little bumps spread across his flesh.

A rat. He hated rats. He lifted his feet off the ground. 'Shoo,' he said softly. 'Scat.'

The rat scurried into a hole.

The minutes ticked by. Mr Simpkin sat watching for the rat but there was no sign of it. After a while he noticed more numbered graffiti. There was another piece of writing scrawled above the toilet-roll holder. It said:

4. ROCK'N'ROLL.

More jokes. He stared at the toilet-roll holder. It moved. He was sure that it moved. It gave a little jiggle.

Mr Simpkin shook with fear. Something strange was going on. He wanted to get out of this loo. Someone was playing jokes. And they weren't funny.

5

The toilet-roll holder began to jig. Back and forward. Up and down in a regular beat like a musician tapping his feet. It was jigging to silent music. It was beating out a tune. Mr Simpkin thought that he had heard it somewhere before. He was sure it was an old rock'n'roll number.

Without warning the jigging stopped.

Even though it was cold Mr Simpkin began to sweat. He was trapped like a rat in a crazy toilet.

He tried to figure it out. There was something strange about the writing on the wall. The first bit of numbered graffiti had said 'this joint closes at five'. And it had. On the dot. Nothing strange about that.

But the next one had pointed to 'the best seat in the house'. And it was the best seat. And the weirdest.

And then there was the 'no standing' sign. Forcing him to sit down. And what about the 'rock'n'roll' paper holder? It had started to rock'n'roll. It really had. Or was it just the wind? Or the water pipes shaking it?

Mr Simpkin had the feeling that he was going out of his mind. But then – if you are mad, you are the only one who doesn't know. And he was wondering whether or not he was sane. So he couldn't be mad. Or could he?

'Get a grip of yourself, man,' he whispered. His voice echoed around the lonely lavatory.

There was only one explanation. He tried to push the thought from his mind. He tried to stop thinking it. But the unwanted thought winkled its way into his brain. The graffiti was coming true. Acting itself out. Everything written on the wall was happening.

Mr Simpkin's hands began to shake. He rushed over to the locked gate and shook the bars. 'Help,' he called. 'Get me out of here.'

Water dripped and pinged but there was no reply.

He shouted and yelled. Kicked and screamed. But the empty night gave no answer.

Slowly he walked back to the velvet seat and sat down. He closed his eyes tightly. He didn't want to read the walls. He was too terrified to think about it.

A sound disturbed the silence. A hinge creaked loudly. Mr Simpkin opened his eyes and stared. The cubicle door slowly swung outwards.

6

There was a big space underneath the door. Just above the gap was scrawled:

5. *BEWARE OF LIMBO DANCERS.*

Another joke. But Mr Simpkin didn't laugh. His lips were frozen in a bewildered grin. His tongue was stuck to the roof of his dry mouth. His eyes bulged.

Music began to play. It sounded as if a whole band was playing inside the toilet. An invisible orchestra. He knew the tune. 'The Limbo Rock'. Da da da da da da da da da. Da da da da da da da da. It surged and swelled. Rocking and rollicking.

Suddenly a dancing, swaying line of people filled the empty building. They seemed to appear from nowhere. They wore crazy hats and blew party squeakers. They clapped their hands and kicked their feet. The line swayed and swerved and approached the cubicle door.

One by one the partygoers leaned back on their heels and passed under the open door. They ignored Mr Simpkin. He was like an uninvited ghost at a banquet. He sat still, terrified on his velvet seat as the line came back for another limbo. Without warning a gust of wind slammed the door. It banged loudly. Mr Simpkin winced and closed his eyes. When he opened them, the line of dancers had disappeared. He was alone once more. Silence replaced the music.

What was going on? What? What? What? Was this a nightmare? Every bit of numbered graffiti was coming true. What else was written there? People wrote terrible things on toilet walls.

He looked above his head:

6. *DROWNED IN THE DUNNY AT DAWN.*

Mr Simpkin shrieked. He jumped off his velvet seat and stared down into the water. 'No,' he shrieked. 'Not that. No, no, no.'

He ran over to the corner. As far away from the pan as he could get. He squatted down on the floor, curling up into a tight ball. He closed his eyes and refused to read any more. He tried to sleep. So that he could wake up from this dreadful nightmare.

But sleep wouldn't come. He crouched there, not moving, as the minutes and hours ticked by. His stomach rumbled. His legs were stiff. He thought his ordeal would never end. But at last the first rays of sunlight crept through the iron gate.

Dawn.

Mr Simpkin shook. He looked around for a weapon. There was nothing.

7

His eyes rested on a shape moving along the top of the wall of the empty cubicle. It was the rat. It crept forwards. Mr Simpkin crouched down. What if the rat leapt at him? Flew through the air with bared fangs?

It was better not to wait. He stood up and waved his arms. 'Shoo,' he yelled. 'Scat. Buzz off.'

The rat was startled. It reared up on its back legs. And slipped. It fell, tumbling into the velvet toilet. With the speed of a cobra, Mr Simpkin lunged across the floor and pressed the diamond button.

The rat disappeared in a gurgling flush.

Mr Simpkin slumped down. The writing had come true. The rat had drowned at dawn.

He wondered what else was written. It was no use putting it off any longer. He searched the walls for more numbered graffiti. And found one more piece. It simply said:

7. *THERE'S NO PLACE LIKE HOME.*

Without warning there was a clang. A key turned

in a lock. The iron gate was thrown open.

Mr Simpkin took one last look around his prison. And fled. There was no sign of a gatekeeper. Who had opened the door? He didn't know. Or care. He was free. He fled across the park.

'There's no place like home. You can say that again,' he thought to himself. If he hurried he might get back before Gobble woke up. He could make Gobble's breakfast especially tasty. He would hand over his pay packet. Gobble might forgive him for taking a night off. If not, well, he would just have to take whatever punishment was dealt out.

Anything would be better than spending another night in that terrifying toilet. Running away had been a big mistake.

He was hungry. Starving. After he had fed Gobble he would make himself a nice meal of . . .

Sheep's eyes.

Mr Simpkin stopped running. He walked slowly with heavy steps. His shoulders were hunched as if he carried a great burden. Suddenly he stopped. And turned. He started to run back across the grass.

The gate of the toilet was still open. He hurried inside and looked at his watch. Two minutes to seven. He felt inside his pocket. And found what he was looking for – a blunt pencil.

He took it out and carefully wrote on the toilet wall:

8. *GOBBLE DISAPPEARS FOREVER AT SEVEN O'CLOCK.*

Mr Simpkin hurried home. He burst into the flat. 'Gobble,' he called. 'Are you there, Gobble?'

There was no reply.

His brother was nowhere to be seen.

Cry Baby

Okay, I shouldn't have done it. I was stupid.

'Who is responsible for that?' said Mr Kempsy. He was pointing at the pin board.

'Cry Baby,' said one of the kids.

'Stand up, Gavin,' said Mr Kempsy.

He needn't have asked me to stand up. I'd been standing up all week. I faced the class. Outside the window I could see the desert stretching off into the distance. I wished I was there. 'Did you do that drawing?' said Mr Kempsy. He knew it was mine. That's why he was asking. I nodded my head. 'Now,' he said, 'tell us how you did it.'

Everyone looked at the wall where my picture was pinned. I had called it 'Elephant Ears' because that's what it looked like.

'Well,' said Mr Kempsy. 'We're waiting.' He knew

how I did it. Otherwise he wouldn't have been asking.

I breathed deeply. 'Last week I went into the staff room after school,' I said.

'Yes,' he growled.

'Then I pulled down my pants, sat on the photo-copier and pressed the button.'

Well, you have never heard anything like it. The class cracked up. They laughed till the tears ran down their faces. I just stood there feeling stupid. My face was red and so was my burnt bottom.

Mr Kempsy didn't laugh though. He suspended me from school for a week.

Mum didn't laugh either. She went on and on and on about it. The way parents always do.

That's the worst of being a kid. You never know when you are going to cop it. You can get into trouble at any time. One minute everything is fine and then 'boom' – you are dead meat. Things can turn nasty just when you least expect it.

Like what happened the next day after the elephant ears and Mr Kempsy. Let me put you in the picture. I had to stay home from school. Mum wouldn't talk to me so I moped around feeling awful. After she went out I did a whole heap of jobs without even being asked. I tried to make up for what I had done. When I had finished the washing-up I stood in the lounge and watched TV.

2

Mum had left her new writing pad on the coffee table. Now that might not seem like much to you but you have to remember that she had once told me this: 'Gavin, you are never to touch this writing pad. It was Aunt Nellie's and there are only a few pages left. They are precious pages.'

Aunt Nellie had drowned when she paddled her canoe in front of a ship carrying rainforest timber. The boat broke her canoe in half and she was never seen again. Mum kept Aunt Nellie's picture on the kitchen wall and she often stood staring at it.

Anyway, like I said, I was standing there watching TV – a movie called *The Old Man and the Sea*.

The writing pad was on the coffee table. It was made of delicate, thin paper with a design on the top. Trees – a lovely forest spreading across the top of the page. I wanted a closer look. I didn't want to write in it. I didn't want to tear out a page. I just wanted a look. There was nothing wrong with that really. Was there?

So I picked it up and sat down.

Now you are going to find out why they call me Cry Baby. See, all week I had been forgetting about my burnt behind. Every time I sat down it hurt so much that tears sprang into my eyes.

As you have probably guessed, the tears started to flow. Right down onto Mum's special writing pad. Even though I jumped up straight away the whole thing was drenched. I mopped up the tears but it was no good. The trees were all bent and twisted and the leaves were running off the branches. The paper was wet and stained.

My heart started to thump. This was it. This was death. I was gone. First the elephant ears and now the paper. Mum was going to kill me. I thought about rushing down the street to buy another pad. But I knew that I would never find one. Aunt Nellie's pad was as old as the hills.

My stomach felt weak. Any time now Mum would come back. I went outside to see if there was any sign of her. Grandpop was in the front yard packing up his truck for another venture into the desert. 'What are you looking for this time?' I asked.

He held up a photo. 'The best one,' he said. 'The water-holding frog.' He was so excited that his hands were shaking. All his life he had wanted to find a specimen of the water-holding frog. His old face was wrinkled by a huge smile. His eyes twinkled. This was going to be the tenth trip looking for this frog. I was scared that he was going to die before he found one. I could feel tears welling up in my eyes because the thought of it was so sad.

I tried to get my mind off it by thinking of something else. That wasn't hard. I just thought about what Mum was going to do to me when she came home.

'Did I ever tell you about the water-holding frog?' Grandpop asked. I nodded but he started telling me again anyway. 'This frog,' he said, 'lives in the desert. Before the summer comes it fills itself up with water and burrows into the ground. It can stay down there for years and years, waiting for the rain. Then, one day the rains come. Water seeps through the sand and wakes up the sleeping frog. It burrows out and sings in the rain. Wonderful. Marvellous.' He was all excited. His whiskers were fairly bristling with joy.

Grandpop slammed the door of the truck and took out his keys. 'Tell your mother that I'll be back the day after tomorrow,' he said in his croaky old voice. He jumped into the truck and started up the engine.

A cloud of dust was approaching in the distance. It was Mum's Land Rover. I felt sick inside. I couldn't face her.

3

Okay, I shouldn't have done it. I was stupid.

But I did. I pulled open the back door of Grandpop's truck and climbed in. I knelt down and hid under a blanket. I was careful not to sit on my burnt bottom, I can tell you that. The truck was full of exploring equipment. A curtain was drawn across behind Grandpop's seat. I felt quite safe snuggled down among the tents and pans. The roar of Mum's Land Rover went by outside.

I had to stay hidden until we reached our destination. If Grandpop found me before we got there he'd just turn back. The truck bumped and jolted. It was hot and I started to get thirsty.

Grandpop started to sing. He was making up the words as he went. It was a sad little song about the water-holding frog. It told how the raindrops fell and woke up the sleeping frogs. 'Oh, what a sight that would be,' he said to himself.

Suddenly, more than anything else in the world, I wanted to help Grandpop find a water-holding frog before he died. Being in Mum's bad books didn't seem important at all any more. I was so excited that I even forgot how thirsty I was.

The truck bumped on and on. I lay on my stomach in the back, dreaming that I would be the one to find the water-holding frog. Grandpop would be happy. Mum would be happy too because she loved Grandpop so much. She probably wouldn't even go crook at me about running away or ruining the writing pad. I had to find a water-holding frog. For everyone's sake.

Just then I heard a blast from a horn. I peeped out of the back and saw two blokes in a hotted-up car. It was a red Ford with big, fat tyres. The driver was trying to make Grandpop go faster. The dirt road was narrow and they couldn't get past. They were really mean-looking guys. The driver was covered in tattoos. The bloke next to him was picking his nose and glaring at us at the same time.

Poor old Grandpop. 'All right, all right,' he said in a trembling voice. 'I'm going as fast as I can.' I could hear him through the curtain that he had stretched behind the front seat. He couldn't see me staring out of the back.

But the two men in the Ford could.

Okay, I shouldn't have done it. I was stupid.

But I just couldn't help myself. I bent one finger and held the knuckle up under my nose. It looked like my finger was going right up inside my nostril. Then I twisted my wrist and with my other hand, pointed at the guy who was picking his nose.

Well, he went right off. His face turned red. The big Ford suddenly lurched off the road and tore past in a swirl of dust. The driver blasted his horn and cut us off. The truck bumped and skidded on the edge of the road. For a second I thought we were going to turn over.

But we didn't. Somehow or other Grandpop managed to keep the truck on the road. 'Idiots,' he yelled as the Ford disappeared into the distance.

I sure hoped we weren't going to meet those blokes again.

4

My throat was parched. There was a water barrel in the back but I couldn't get to it without shifting some boxes. Grandpop might hear me.

After another four hours the truck stopped. I heard Grandpop get out. I peeped through a window and saw that we were at one of those lonely little petrol stations in the middle of the desert. A big sign said LAST STOP BEFORE ALICE SPRINGS. Behind the sign I saw a red Ford parked in the shade.

Grandpop started filling the truck with petrol.

This was my chance to get a drink. The water was in a large drum with a tap at the bottom. I grabbed a mug and filled it up. Boy, was I thirsty. I drank mug after mug full. I was just filling my fourth mug when I heard shouting.

I peeped outside. The big tattooed guy and his mate were pushing Grandpop around. They had his hat and were throwing it to each other. Poor old Grandpop had no one to help him. Except me. I forgot all about the water that was pouring into the mug. I just dropped everything and leaped out of the car.

Grandpop jumped and hopped like a little kid, trying to get his hat back. He was really old and I could see it was hard for him to move. His breath came out in noisy wheezes. Sweat was pouring down his cheeks. Or was it tears?

Now I'm quite good at basketball, if I do say so myself. I took a flying leap up onto the back of the tattooed one and snatched the hat. He fell down in the dust onto his knees.

Grandpop was amazed to see me. 'Gavin,' he yelled. Half happy, half mad.

The two big guys came towards us. They were not half happy and they were not half mad. They were completely furious. They started to walk towards us. We backed away.

But at that exact moment the owner of the garage came out. He was the biggest man I had ever seen. His legs were like tree trunks. His fists were like boulders. 'What's going on?' he said.

'Nothing,' said the nose picker. Both men headed towards their car muttering beneath their breath. As they drove off I held my knuckle up to my nose for one more time. They saw me but they kept going. I felt quite safe standing there with a giant next to me. Lucky for us we never saw them again.

Grandpop gave me a big lecture but I could see that he was glad to have me there. He went inside the garage and rang Mum. I waited outside feeling nervous. After a bit Grandpop came out. 'She said you can come with me,' he said.

'Did she say anything else?' I asked.

He gave me a wink. 'She said she's busy writing letters on her new pad.'

Whew. What a relief. She wasn't angry with me any more. Now we could get on with it. And find a water-holding frog.

It was good not to be in any trouble. It was good not to feel guilty for messing things up. I climbed into the back of the truck and knelt behind Grandpop's seat. We headed off into the burning desert which was nearly as hot as my burning bottom. Neither of us knew that I had left the water tap turned on in the back.

5

Grandpop was so pleased to have me. 'That water-holding frog will amaze you,' he said. 'The rain falls after the drought. It soaks into the ground. And the little frog digs its way up.' He was so happy. It was enough to bring tears to your eyes.

I wasn't so sure though. I looked out at the bleached desert. It was the middle of summer. 'How will you find a frog?' I said. 'They'll all be underground.'

'Dig,' he said. 'The ground will be rock-hard and digging is the only way.'

We turned off the main road and headed across the hot red earth. Spinifex and mulga bushes were the only plants in the barren soil. Grandpop often stopped to check his compass. Each time he did we had a swig from his water bottle. You sure got thirsty out there in the middle of nowhere. I loved the feel of that cool water trickling down my throat.

After four hours we reached the waterhole. I say waterhole but of course, at that time of the year it was only a claypan. Just a shallow, dry hole.

The truck bumped to a stop. 'Just in time,' said Grandpop. 'The radiator is boiling.' Sure enough, clouds of steam came whooshing out of the bonnet. 'It doesn't matter,' he said. 'I've brought plenty of water.'

We went around to the back of the truck to unpack.

You know what I said about never knowing when you were going to be in trouble? Well, when Grandpop found out that we had no water, it was worse than ever. Once again I had mucked things up.

He didn't go crook because I left the tap on. He didn't tell me off. He just stood there looking very worried. Very worried indeed. In a way, it was worse than being yelled at. I felt terrible. It was all my fault.

'What will we do?' I said.

'We stay here,' replied Grandpop. 'The first rule in the desert is to stay with your vehicle. Someone will come and look for us.'

'No one knows where we are,' I said.

'They know roughly where we are,' he said. 'Anyway, we don't have any choice. The car is no good without water. And we don't have a drop to spare.'

I tried to cheer him up a bit. 'We can look for the water-holding frog while we wait,' I said.

He shook his head. 'We have to conserve our energy. All we can do is wait for help without moving too much.'

I felt so guilty. Now he was never going to find his water-holding frog. And it was all my fault.

We put up a canvas shelter on the side of the truck to stop the heat of the sun. Grandpop handed me the water bottle. 'Take two swigs,' he said. I held back my head and took two swigs. I couldn't have taken three swigs even if I'd wanted to. There was none left. Grandpop had given me the last of the water. That's the sort of bloke he was.

6

I wondered how long we could last with nothing to drink. Grandpop would go first. I was young and strong. He was old and weak. What if I lived and he died? I couldn't bear the thought of it.

Hours passed. Night crept up. Mosquitoes whined. Things moved in the night. The moon rose. It became cold and we wrapped ourselves in blankets.

The next morning it grew hot quickly. My mouth was dry and dusty. I could hardly swallow. Grandpop dozed and mumbled. He seemed to be off in a dream.

The sun rose higher and higher. 'Frog. Little water-holding frog,' mumbled Grandpop. His eyes were wild. He didn't seem to know what was going on. The heat was getting to him. He crawled on his hands and knees into the middle of the claypan. He started scratching at the sand with his bent fingers. 'Frog, little frog,' he croaked.

I gently led him back to the shade. 'I'll get you a frog,' I said.

Only one thought filled my mind. Find Grandpop a water-holding frog. I didn't care about being rescued. I didn't care whether I lived or died. Grandpop was off his head but it didn't make any difference. All I wanted was to put one of those frogs into his hand.

Everything was my fault. He would die soon, without water, I knew that. I had to grant his life-long wish. I had to find one of those frogs.

I grabbed a shovel and trudged into the middle of the claypan. I whacked the point down into the ground. Wham. It was as hard as rock. The shock hurt my fingers.

The hot sand shimmered. Flies buzzed around my eyes. Dust covered my skin. But on I dug. On and on. Each time I hit the ground with the shovel I collected a small pile of sand. 'Frog,' I said. 'Little frog, where are you?'

But there was no answer. The water-holding frogs were all buried deep, waiting for the first drops of water to fall and wake them from their long sleep.

My fingers started to bleed. Large blisters grew and burst on my palms. I had managed to dig out a hole about the size of a shallow bath. But still no frog. It was no good. I would never find one. My tongue felt like a piece of shrivelled leather.

Grandpop lay there in the shade. I could tell he was still alive because his chest was going up and down. But he didn't have much longer to go. Not without water. I had to find a water-holding frog before it was too late. I couldn't give up.

Grandpop mumbled to himself 'Little frog, little water-holding frog.'

I wrapped a rag around my blistered hand and started to dig again. Painfully. Slowly. Bending, scraping, digging only a few grains at a time. My head started to spin. It was no good. I just couldn't lift the shovel any more.

7

I tried to dig with my grazed fingers but they made no impression on the baked ground.

It was useless. I couldn't go on. I stood and looked at the empty horizon. Grandpop would never get his water-holding frog. He would die without his dream coming true. And it was all my fault. It was so sad.

Okay, I shouldn't have done it. I was stupid.

I sat down in despair. Wow. Did my bottom sting. It was still red and sore. The pain was terrible. Tears streamed down my nose and plopped onto the hard ground. A regular waterfall of tears. A little wet patch formed on the sand just beneath my cheek.

Suddenly, in the middle of the damp sand, a small green leg appeared. And then another.

My tears had woken a water-holding frog from its sleep. Two eyes blinked at me. Two wonderful, wonderful eyes.

'I've got one, Grandpop,' I screamed. 'I've got one.' Gently I picked up the glistening frog. I walked over to Grandpop and placed the tiny creature in his hand.

I wouldn't have believed that one little frog could have had such an effect. Grandpop leaned up and gave the biggest grin I had ever seen. He looked at me with love in his smile. Love for me. And the frog. We both had tears in our eyes.

It was such a magic moment that neither of us noticed the storm clouds gathering. We just sat looking at that frog until the first raindrops fell. And the pool began to fill. The songs of a thousand frogs filled the air.

It was a real downpour. The heavens seemed to be weeping as I stood there and rubbed my behind. 'Cry, baby,' I said to the sky. 'Cry, baby, cry.'

Ex Poser

There are two rich kids in our form. Sandra Morris and Ben Fox. They are both snobs. They think they are too good for the rest of us. Their parents have big cars and big houses. Both of them are quiet. They keep to themselves. I guess they don't want to mix with the ruffians like me.

Ben Fox always wears expensive gym shoes and the latest fashions. He thinks he is good-looking with his blue eyes and blond hair. He is a real poser.

Sandra Morris is the same. And she knows it. Blue eyes and blonde hair too. Skin like silk. Why do some kids get the best of everything?

Me, I landed pimples. I've used everything I can on them. But still they bud and grow and burst. Just when you don't want them to. It's not fair.

Anyway, today I have the chance to even things up. Boffin is bringing along his latest invention – a lie detector. Sandra Morris is the victim. She agreed to try it out because everyone knows that she would never tell a lie. What she doesn't know is that Boffin and I are going to ask her some very embarrassing questions.

Boffin is a brain. His inventions always work. He is smarter than the teachers. Everyone knows that. And now he has brought along his latest effort. A lie detector.

He tapes two wires to Sandra's arm. 'It doesn't hurt,' he says. 'But it is deadly accurate.' He switches on the machine and a little needle swings into the middle of the dial. 'Here's a trial question,' he says. 'Are you a girl?'

Sandra nods.

'You have to say yes or no,' he says.

'Yes,' replies Sandra. The needle swings over to TRUTH. Maybe this thing really works. Boffin gives a big grin.

'This time tell a lie,' says Boffin. 'Are you a girl?' he asks again.

Sandra smiles with that lovely smile of hers. 'No,' she says. A little laugh goes up but then all the kids in the room gasp. The needle points to LIE. This lie detector is a terrific invention.

'Okay,' says Boffin. 'You only have seven questions, David. The batteries will go flat after another seven questions.' He sits down behind his machine and twiddles the knobs.

This is going to be fun. I am going to find out a little bit about Sandra Morris and Ben Fox. It's going to be very interesting. Very interesting indeed.

I ask my first question. 'Have you ever kissed Ben Fox?'

Sandra goes red. Ben Fox goes red. I have got them this time. I am sure they have something going between them. I will expose them.

'No,' says Sandra. Everyone cranes their neck to see what the lie detector says. The needle points to TRUTH.

This is not what I expected. And I only have six questions left. I can't let her off the hook. I am going to expose them both.

'Have you ever held his hand?'

Again she says, 'No.' And the needle says TRUTH. I am starting to feel guilty. Why am I doing this?

I try another tack. 'Are you in love?' I ask.

A red flush starts to crawl up her neck. I am feeling really mean now. Fox is blushing like a sunset.

'Yes,' she says. The needle points to TRUTH.

I shouldn't have let the kids talk me into doing this. I decide to put Sandra and Ben out of their agony. I won't actually name him. I'll spare her that. 'Is he in this room?' I say.

She looks at the red Ben Fox. 'Yes,' she says. The needle points to TRUTH.

'Does he have blue eyes?' I ask.

'No,' she says.

'Brown?' I say.

'No,' she says again.

I don't know what to say next. I look at each kid in the class very carefully. Ben Fox has blue eyes. I was sure that she loved him.

'This thing doesn't work,' I say to Boffin. 'I can't see one kid who doesn't have either blue eyes or brown eyes.'

'We can,' says Boffin. They are all looking at me.

I can feel *my* face turning red now. I wish I could sink through the floor but I get on with my last question. 'Is he an idiot?' I ask.

Sandra is very embarrassed. 'Yes,' she says in a voice that is softer than a whisper. 'And he has green eyes.'

Sloppy Jalopy

My sister Helen looked around the schoolyard and then pointed to my ear. 'You're mad wearing an earring to school,' she said.

'Smacka Johns,' said a voice behind me. 'Come here at once.'

It was Ms Cranch, the vice principal. She held out her hand. 'Give me that earring.'

'But it's only a sleeper,' I said as I handed it over.

'No jewellery is allowed at school,' she snapped.

Before I could get another word out she turned round and headed off towards her office with my earring.

'I told you,' said Helen.

'She's the crabbiest teacher I ever met,' I grumbled. 'I wonder what she does with the earrings. She must have millions of 'em.'

'She wears them,' said Helen. 'I saw her wearing mine down the street once.'

'She wouldn't,' I said scornfully. 'Even crotchety old Cranch wouldn't nick stuff from kids.'

All day I thought about my earring. I got madder. And madder. And madder. By the time school was over I had made a decision. There was only one thing to do. Buy another earring and wear it to school as a protest. Teachers aren't allowed to steal from kids.

I went straight home and strode into the lounge. 'Dad,' I said. 'Can you take me into town? I want to buy a new earring.'

Dad smiled. 'Sure,' he said. 'I'm just on my way out.'

Earrings didn't worry Dad. He used to wear one himself once. He's not your regular sort of dad. He is always doing crazy, wild things. To be perfectly honest, sometimes he is a bit of an embarrassment.

We walked out to the car. Dad had always wanted a sports car but he couldn't afford it. So he cut the top off our Holden and now we could only use it when it wasn't raining.

On the way to town I complained about the car. 'I don't know what you're going on about,' said Dad.

'This is a fabulous car. No one else in town has got one like it. Who wants to be like everyone else?'

I smiled. He was right. I didn't want to be like everyone else. Little did I know that in a very short time my wish was going to come true in a big way.

2

We finally reached town and Dad pulled up behind a filthy-looking tanker truck. He pointed to a shop. 'There,' he said. 'They sell earrings.'

The shop was dingy and cobwebbed. It looked spooky inside. I felt a bit nervous. 'I've changed my mind,' I said to Dad. 'I don't like the look of this place.'

'Rubbish,' said Dad. 'Hurry up, I've got my own shopping to do.' He pushed me through the door into the shop.

I banged straight into an enormous man dressed in shorts and a blue singlet. He clutched an earring between his fingers. He smelt terrible. Awful. 'Watch it,' he growled. He brushed past me and swept through the door.

'Sorry,' I mumbled.

An old man with an incredibly wrinkled face was serving at the counter.

'I'm looking for an earring,' I said.

The shopkeeper smiled at me. 'I usually only sell them in pairs,' he said. 'But that gentleman talked me into letting him have just one. You can have the matching one if you want. They were second-hand. I bought them from a palm reader.'

It was just what I wanted so I handed over five dollars. Then I put the earring in my pocket. We walked out into the street and jumped into the Holden.

A horrible stench filled the air. It was coming from the tanker truck in front.

Straight away I knew what it was. Newman's Pond. The Council had been emptying it and taking the contents to their depot. It was the most putrid pond in the whole world. Drains from the fertiliser works, the fish factory and the oil refinery poured into it. Everything was dead for metres around. Green slime covered the surface. Stifling fumes bubbled into the fetid air. Horrible lumps floated in the slime.

The Council workers had to wear gas masks while they were sucking the squelching goo into the trucks. The sludge in that tanker was the stuff of nightmares. *My* nightmares as it turned out.

The guy in the blue singlet drove the truck out onto the road. We followed in our convertible. I was longing for fresh air. But I didn't get it.

Little brown flecks flicked off the truck and onto our windscreen. Dad turned on the wipers but they only made things worse. A foul smear made it almost impossible to see. The spattering turned into a shower. Filthy specks of putrid liquid covered us like freckles.

'What a nerve,' yelled Dad. 'Look what he's doing to my car.'

I wasn't worried about the car. I was worried about me. I was splotted with dreadful droplets. I shuddered to think where they came from.

The back of the truck had a large valve for connection to a pipe. I could just imagine what had been sucked in through it.

Dad beeped the horn. 'Pull over,' he screamed. 'You idiot. You're polluting the whole town.'

I myself would not have called the driver an idiot. Not a big guy like that. But Dad never thinks of the consequences. He pulled out next to the truck and shook his fist at the guy in the blue singlet. 'Pull over, you fool,' Dad yelled through his brown smeared lips.

The truck lurched over to the side of the road and stopped.

3

The driver stepped out. Dad stepped out. I did not step out.

'You're flicking foul muck all over the street,' said Dad. 'Tighten that valve up.' Dad pointed to a wheel on top of the valve.

'Did you call me an idiot?' said the driver. He was an awfully big bloke.

'Well,' said Dad, trying to laugh. 'Look what you've done.' They stared at our spattered car. I pretended I wasn't there.

'An idiot, eh,' said the driver. 'An idiot, am I? I guess I'm so dumb that I couldn't even tighten the valve up properly.' He jumped up on the back of the truck and began turning the wheel. 'Oh dear,' he said. 'I seem to be turning it the wrong way.'

'Aghhhh . . .' I screamed. 'No. Mercy. No, no, no.'

But I was too late. An enormous jet of bilious brown sludge hit me in the head. It flooded. It surged. It filled the car to the top of the doors and poured down onto the street.

I gagged and gasped in the middle of my own private cesspool. Horrible lumps floated by. A rotting fish head swirled by in its own polluted sea.

Our car had been transformed into an ecological disaster.

I fumbled for the door handle and was swept out onto the footpath by the unspeakable flow.

My ears and eyes and nose were choked with the filth. I coughed and spluttered and dragged myself across the footpath. People on the street jumped back in horror. They held handkerchiefs to their noses.

They glared at me as if I was a monster spewed up from dark and hideous places. I stood up and shook myself like a dog coming out of the water. A moaning sigh of horror swept across the passers-by. They fell back in fear as my spray scattered in the breeze.

The smell was terrible. I stank like a sewer. I dripped with dung. Foulness fell like melting manure from my putrid skin. I choked with each tortured breath.

The guy in the blue singlet thought it was funny. He started laughing. He turned off the terrible flow, jumped in his truck and drove off.

Dad just stood there staring at his contaminated car and shaking his head.

'Help,' I gurgled. Brown bubbles formed on the end of my nose as I spoke. I felt weak. The fumes were making my head spin. Suddenly my brown world turned to black. I collapsed on the footpath.

4

When I awoke most of the muck had gone. Dad stood squirting me with a hose which the butcher had lent him. 'You'll be okay,' said Dad with a grin. 'It's all part of the rich pageant of life.' He took a deep breath, blew up his cheeks and started to hose out the car. Every now and then he dashed away and gulped in fresh air.

But there was no fresh air for me. I stank. I staggered over to a flower-box outside a shop. I swear that the flowers wilted in front of my eyes. People crossed the street to avoid the mad father flushing out his car. And his horrible, stinking son.

It was a hot day and a lot of the gunk had become baked on the car. Dad couldn't get it off. The butcher approached with a handkerchief over his nose. 'Look,' he said. 'You'll have to get that thing out of here. I'm losing business.'

Dad opened the car door. 'Get in,' he said to me.

'You're joking,' I gasped. 'It'll never start.'

'Get in,' he said again.

I did as I was told. I squeezed into the sodden, foul seat. Dad turned over the engine. It started first go. I couldn't believe it. 'They don't build 'em like this any more,' Dad said with a smile.

We set off down the road throwing a brown shower out behind us. Talk about embarrassing. Now it was us who were polluting the neighbourhood. The following cars tooted and bipped. Drivers shook their fists at us as freckles of foulness spattered their windscreens.

'Step on it,' I said to Dad. 'I can't take much more of this.' Chitty Chitty Bang Bang had nothing on this car.

After what seemed about ten years Dad finally reached our house. 'You go in and have a shower,' he said. 'I'm taking the car into town to get it steam-cleaned.'

I was already halfway to the door before he'd finished talking. A shower. Oh, how I longed for a shower. I stayed under the water for at least an hour. I scrubbed. And rubbed. I soaped and soaked. I had to get every bit of gunk off my skin.

This was pollution of the worst type. Who knew

what chemicals had been dumped in that pond?

At last I jumped out of the water. I dried myself and put on my new earring. Then I examined my reflection in the mirror. Something was wrong. Maybe the sludge had seeped into my skin. I sniffed myself all over like a dog. I didn't seem to smell. But something was different. My skin tingled. It felt strange. Still, after what had happened it was no wonder.

I walked down to the kitchen. That's when everything started to go wrong.

5

A movement in the corner caught my eye. Someone had thrown a used tissue there. It was flapping in the breeze. Except there was no breeze. Without warning, the tissue sort of flapped and twirled and then flew across the room. It plastered itself onto my face.

I gave a little scream and tore it off. It twisted and squirmed in my hand. I screwed it into a ball and threw it down on the floor. The tissue bounced and then shot back and stuck itself onto my nose.

I heard a noise. 'Dad,' I yelled. But it wasn't Dad.

An empty sardine tin slid towards me. It sped across the floor and attached itself to my right foot. I pulled it off and threw it into the corner where it stayed for about half a second. Then it sped straight back to its place on my foot.

I rubbed my eyes. This was crazy. First the tissue and now the sardine tin. Sticking to me like glue. What was going on? I pulled on my clothes like a crazy man.

Something had happened to me. Something awful. I tried to peer at myself in the mirror. But before I could even catch a glimpse of my face my vision was blotted out. About twenty tissues flew out of the waste-paper basket and covered my face.

Hairs trapped in the plug-hole of the sink started to move. They twirled and then, like flicked rubber bands, shot through the air and stuck to my jumper.

My mind swirled. Was I going crazy? Was this really happening?

It was.

Rubbish. I was attracting rubbish. Like a magnet.

'Newman's Pond,' I said to myself. 'The stinking waste has made me magnetic. Filth is attracting filth.'

A gnarled old toothbrush swooped towards me. Two empty drink bottles followed.

117

I looked around for somewhere to hide. By the door was our phone box. One of those old-fashioned red ones that used to be on street corners. I had laughed when Dad bought it. But now I wasn't laughing.

I bolted into the phone box and slammed the door behind me. I made it just in time. The bottles glued themselves to the glass. The toothbrush tried to jiggle its way under the door.

I tried to think. I was shivering with fear. Rubbish of every sort was seeking me out. My life was in danger. I could be buried. Suffocated. Bits of fluff and dust were wriggling under the door. Spent matches and bottle tops followed and splotted onto my knees.

My brain wouldn't work. 'Think,' I said to myself. 'Think.'

I was sure that the water from Newman's Pond had done something to my skin. That man in the blue singlet. He was responsible. He lived with that stuff every day. He must have some sort of soap to cure it. I grabbed the phone book and flipped through the pages. 'South Barwon Council Depot,' l said to myself. 'Got it.'

My fingers fumbled with the dial. I heard the

phone ringing at the other end. 'Come on,' I said. 'Come on, come on.'

But there was no answer. The man with the blue singlet was probably out in the yard emptying the revolting contents of his truck.

The phone box was almost completely covered in garbage. Junk was hurtling across the room and flapping on the glass as if it was alive. At any moment the glass might break.

It was time to make a run for it. I was just about to force the door open when my heart froze in terror.

Our garbage can was rattling. It jiggled and wiggled as if demons inside were trying to burst out.

I turned back to the phone book and looked up the taxi company. I dialled with a shaking hand. 'Address?' said a voice.

'Fifteen Henry Street,' I gasped.

'Going to?' asked the voice.

'South Barwon,' I said. 'The Council Depot.'

'Please wait,' said a voice on the other end of the phone.

'Hurry,' I yelled. 'It's an emergency.'

'Ten minutes,' said the voice.

I stared out of the phone box at the bulging bin over by the sink. At any moment it might burst.

I could be trapped in the phone box if I stayed much longer.

6

More and more rubbish flattened itself against the glass door. A newspaper flew across the room and flapped over to join the attack. The phone box door was creaking and cracking under the strain. There wasn't much time left.

'Hurry,' I shouted. 'Hurry.'

A horn sounded from outside. I groaned with relief. A pane cracked next to my ear. Glass and junk exploded into the phone box. I charged out of the house. Our garbage bin rattled and jumped as I ran past it. Debris followed me as I fled.

I yanked open the taxi door and jumped into the back seat. I slammed the door just in time to keep out most of the garbage. 'Where to?' said the taxi driver. He was a little, nervous-looking guy. His eyes nearly bugged out of his head when he saw my coating of junk.

'South Barw . . .' I started to say. I never finished the sentence. The contents of the taxi's ashtray flew through the air straight into my mouth. Filthy cigarette butts, ash and dead matches crammed themselves between my lips. I choked and spluttered and spat them out. They stuck to my face like glue.

'What the . . .' shouted the taxi driver. 'Get out of my . . .'

We both looked out of the window as a loud bang filled the air. The lid had shot off our garbage bin as if it had been dynamited. The contents were bouncing and flying down the path towards us. They smattered onto the back of the taxi and rattled on the rear window.

Plastic bags full of refuse were bouncing our way along the track. 'Quick,' I screamed. 'Quick. Move it or we're history.'

An empty can of cat food hit the taxi window like a mortar shell. With a loud scream the driver put the car into gear and shot forward. Rubbish bounced and banged along after us.

We screeched along the track and out onto the road. The back of the car was piled with cans, paper bags, take-away food boxes and other unmention-ables. Suddenly the driver hit the brakes. A dog. A dog was on the road.

'Don't stop,' I yelled. 'Whatever you do, don't stop. We'll be buried alive.'

The dog was trotting by with a bone in its mouth. The bone started to jiggle. The dog growled and pulled back as if someone was trying to pull the bone out of its mouth. Suddenly the bone shot out of the dog's jaws and flew through the air towards us. The dog charged after it, barking and yelping like crazy. The bone banged onto the back of the car and joined the putrid pile on the boot. The back window blacked out as more and more junk gathered.

The driver raced around the dog and down past the fish factory. 'No, no. Not that,' I screamed. Too late. Hundreds of dead, stinking fish slid out of the factory garbage bins. Flying fish. Dead flying fish. They splattered against the car and flapped on the side windows in their thousands.

'My car. My lovely new car,' groaned the driver.

'Go,' I yelled. 'Faster, faster, faster.'

7

The driver gunned the engine and we raced along the road and out onto the highway. I thought that the rubbish might fall off as we bounced and lurched around the traffic. But no luck. Every piece of rubbish clung on, trying desperately to get inside. Other junk stirred and flew up as we passed but we were too fast for it. Bits of roadside rubbish fell back like cowboys giving up the chase.

'We're safe as long as you keep going,' I shouted over the din of the banging rubbish.

'What happens when we run out of petrol?' he yelled back.

'A man in a blue singlet,' I said. 'At the Council Depot. He knows about it. He must. It's all his fault. Find him.'

'Find the man in the blue singlet,' mumbled the driver. He slowed to take a corner and two mouldy cabbages bounced out of a roadside vegetable stall and lobbed onto the bonnet.

Well, I won't say much about the rest of the journey. Except to say that it was a nightmare. As we moved further into the countryside I thought it would be better. But it wasn't. Every time we slowed down, cow pats in the paddock stirred and flew towards us. They splotted on top of our coating of junk and formed a thick, brown crust.

Only a small clearing on the windscreen remained. The windscreen wipers groaned under the strain. It was me the junk was chasing so I stayed well to the back of the car to attract it away from the windscreen.

Finally we reached a fence with a dirty sign hanging on the gate. South Barwon Council Depot. We only just made it. The car was covered. It was ten times its size. A slowly moving mountain of litter. We stopped. 'I can't see a thing,' said the driver. 'This is the end.'

I looked at the poor guy. He was terrified. 'It's okay,' I told him. 'It's me. I attract rubbish. When I get out it'll all follow me. You'll be okay.'

'What about my taxi?' he asked through the gloom. 'It's covered in filth.'

'It will all drop off and follow me. Don't worry about it,' I said.

He looked at the meter and held out his hand. 'Twenty-five dollars sixty,' he said. 'And it should be two hundred.'

Suddenly I felt weak. I went cold all over. I patted my jeans desperately. I searched every pocket. 'Oh no,' I groaned. 'I've left my wallet at home.'

I closed my eyes in despair. When I opened them I saw that the taxi driver had changed. He wasn't his normal self at all. His face was red. He looked as if he was going to explode.

'What?' he screamed. 'After all this you haven't even got the fare?' He leaned over and grabbed my

T-shirt. He was so mad that he was spitting as he yelled. 'Right. What *have* you got then?'

I fumbled with the strap of my watch. 'You can have this,' I said. 'It's real valuable.'

He looked at my watch scornfully as he strapped it on his wrist. 'Pull the other one,' he growled. Then he pointed to my ear. 'I'll have that as well.'

I was in no position to argue. I took out my new earring and handed it over. He looked in the mirror and threaded it into a hole in his ear. Then he grinned at me – daring me to object.

I had nothing else to give. And I had to get out of there. I heaved open the door of the car and plunged out through the rubbish. I rolled over on the ground like a soldier avoiding bullets. Then I folded my head into my arms and waited for the rubbish to hit.

8

Nothing. Nothing happened. Not for a second or two anyway. I looked down at my clothes. I was as clean as a whistle.

Suddenly a terrible scream came from the taxi. The rubbish was piling into the open door. 'Help,' yelled the driver. 'Help, help help.' He was completely covered in the seething junk. The pieces of rubbish were like rats pouring into a food bin.

I looked around the Depot for something to pull the rubbish away from the poor man. But it was a very clean yard. Strangely clean for that sort of place. There was nothing I could grab.

I ran over to a little shed in the corner of the yard. I tried to get in the door but I couldn't. The shed was filled to the roof with seething junk. 'Help,' came a deep voice from inside. 'Help.'

I'd heard that voice before. It was the guy in the blue singlet.

My head began to spin. The taxi driver was covered in junk. And so was the tanker driver. But the junk wasn't after me any more. Why?

Suddenly it came to me. The earrings. Both earrings came from the same shop. And the same pair. The earrings were attracting the junk, not the sludge from Newman's Pond.

I ran over to the taxi. 'The earring,' I yelled. 'Take off the earring.'

There was muttering and spluttering from inside. Suddenly the junk collapsed. Like cans in a super-market falling, the rubbish tumbled out onto the ground. The taxi driver began to clamber out. He was shaking like a leaf.

I turned my attention to the man in the blue singlet. 'Take off your earring,' I shouted into the junk pile. 'The earrings attract rubbish when you put them on.'

There was more muttering and spluttering as the tanker driver reached up and pulled the earring out. Then without warning, his pile of junk collapsed too. His head poked out of the top like a fairy on a horrible Christmas tree. He climbed out towards us. 'This thing is dangerous,' he said. 'I'm getting rid of it.'

'Me too,' said the taxi driver. They threw back their arms. They were going to hurl the earrings into the paddock.

'No,' I said. 'Don't throw them away.' I picked up an empty jar and held it out towards them.

9

The next day I walked slowly into the school grounds.

'I'm showing these to one of the science teachers,' I said to Helen. 'We could be rich and famous.'

She looked around the schoolyard and then stared

at my jar. 'You're mad bringing more earrings to school,' she said.

'Smacka Johns,' snapped a voice behind me. 'Come here at once.'

It was Ms Cranch, the vice principal. She held out her hand. 'Give me those earrings.'

'But I'm not even wearing them,' I said as I handed over the jar.

'No jewellery is allowed at school,' she said.

Before I could get another word out she turned round and headed off towards her office with my earrings.

'I told you,' said Helen.

I mooched around sulking for about five minutes. Then I suddenly cheered up. All around the yard the garbage cans had started to rattle. They jiggled and wiggled as if demons inside were trying to burst out.

Loud bangs filled the air as the bins burst their lids. I started to laugh as the contents bounced across the yard towards Ms Cranch's office.

Eyes Knows

The people are so far below they look like little pins. I am scared and lonely. If I let go of the ladder I will fall. Down, down, down. Tumbling and turning. I can't bear to think about it. The wind whistles in my hair. The ladder on the crane reaches up towards the sky. I don't know whether to go up. Or down. My fingers are cold and numb. Who can help me? Only my little robot man.

My arm is curled tightly around the ladder but I can just reach him with my hand. I'm scared that I'll fall. I edge the little robot man out of my pocket with trembling fingers. If I drop him I'll never know what to do. 'Little robot man,' I say. 'You are my last chance.' I pull his nose and his eyes begin to spin.

2

It is only four hours since my little robot man started telling me what to do. And it is twenty-four hours since Mum and Dad broke my heart. 'Harry,' said Dad. 'We've got bad news. Your Mum and I are going to split up. We don't love each other any more.' He said a lot of other things but that's the only bit I remember. I ran to Mum and hugged her. My face made hers all wet. Or was it the other way round?

Then I ran to Dad and hugged him. He was crying too. 'What about me?' I said. 'What about me?'

Dad looked at me sadly. 'You have to choose,' he said. 'Mum's going interstate. You can go with her or stay here with me. We're not going to force you. It's up to you. Take a bit of time to think about it. You have to choose.'

How could I make a choice like that? I felt like a nail between two magnets. One magnet pulling me one way. And one the other. I was stuck in the middle.

I looked at my parents. I loved them both. I didn't know what to do. That night there was a terrible storm. I snuggled down inside my blankets. And cried a lot.

In the morning I started to dress myself. There were two pairs of socks. A green pair and a red pair. I couldn't make up my mind which to put on. I put out my hand for the green pair but then stopped. It felt wrong. I reached out for the red ones but that wasn't right either. I couldn't choose.

That's when my little robot man came to the rescue. See, he has two pairs of eyes. They spin like poker machines when you pull his nose. Sometimes the green eyes show and sometimes the red ones. You never know which it's going to be.

I took him down from the shelf and pulled his nose. His eyes spun in a blur. Then they stopped. On green. 'Green eyes – green socks,' I said. I put on my green socks and finished dressing. Then I ran into the kitchen for breakfast.

Dad had already gone to work but Mum was still there. 'Cornflakes or muesli?' she asked. I looked at both packets. I couldn't decide. I reached for the cornflakes but changed my mind. I decided on muesli. But that wasn't right either. What should I do?

There was a quick way out. I pulled the nose of my little robot man. 'Green for cornflakes,' I said. The eyes spun and stopped on red. 'Muesli it is,' I shrugged.

3

I kissed Mum goodbye, grabbed my little robot man and headed for school. I walked slowly. My feet dragged. I really felt down. Before long I was going to have to choose between Mum and Dad. I just couldn't do it. Life is full of terrible choices.

I trudged along, staring at my feet. Suddenly I stopped. There on the footpath was a little furry caterpillar. It was alive, but not moving. It had fallen off the branch of a tree and couldn't get back. Someone would probably stand on it and squash it. All I had to do was bend down, pick it up and put it back on the tree.

I didn't know whether to save the caterpillar or not. I decided to ask my little robot man. I gave his nose a tug and set his eyes spinning. 'Green for yes, red for no,' I said. The eyes spun swiftly and then slowed down. They stopped on green. 'This is your lucky day, caterpillar,' I said. I gently placed it on a leaf on the tree and it started munching straight away.

I felt a bit better. I had saved the caterpillar. My little robot man was good at making choices. I turned the corner and saw an amazing sight. My heart failed for a second. About a thousand caterpillars were wriggling helplessly on the footpath. I guessed that the storm must have knocked them all off the trees.

'Do I save them? Yes or no?' I asked the robot with a trembling voice. The eyes spun. And stopped on green. 'Yes,' I said. 'The answer is yes. Oh no.' I crouched down and started to pick up the caterpillars. Down up, down up. Each one clung gratefully to its leaf and started to munch.

The minutes ticked by. Half an hour passed and I hardly seemed to have saved any of them. I knew I was going to be late for school. My little robot man was getting me into trouble. In the end it took me an hour to put all the caterpillars back on the tree. Every one was munching happily.

I looked at my watch. I was an hour late for school. Mr Hanson would be peering out of his office. He would pounce like a snake as soon as he saw me crossing the yard. I was in big trouble. I looked at my little robot man. 'You've really done it now,' I said. 'That's the last time I ask you to decide anything.' The little robot man was bad luck. I could see that now.

The hairs on the back of my head started to stand up. Someone was watching me. I could just feel it.

I looked around and saw her. Mrs Week, a friend of Mum's. She was on her knees, weeding her garden. She was smiling at me. She called me over with a crooked finger. 'Wait here,' she said in a bright voice. She shuffled inside her house and left me standing alone. She took ages and ages. Finally she came back carrying a little envelope.

'I saw you saving those caterpillars,' she said. 'What a kind boy. No one else would do such a thing. Here's a little reward for you.' She pushed the envelope into my hand.

Should I take it? Yes or no? I wasn't sure. So I pulled the nose on my little robot man. Green. The green eyes blinked at me. It was green for yes. Mrs Week was already walking back inside with a big smile on her face. 'Thanks,' I yelled. 'Thanks a million.'

4

I hurried towards school. I was going to be later than ever. I tore the top off the envelope and looked inside. I stopped walking. Fifty dollars. There was a fifty-dollar note inside. I couldn't believe it.

My little robot man was bringing me incredible

luck. Every time I asked it anything it came up with the right answer. Things worked out.

But what about school? Nothing could save me from the beady eyes of Mr Hanson. Or could it?

I thought of another question. Something to ask my little robot man. 'Shall I wag school? Not go at all?' I pulled his nose. And his eyes stopped on green. Two green eyes telling me to wag it.

This was the way to decide things. This was definitely the best method to find out what to do. Everything my little robot man told me to do worked out right. I slowed down. Some old people were blocking the way. They were waiting outside a take-away hamburger place. A very crabby nurse was bossing them around:

'Don't block the path,' she snapped at a poor old lady. 'Wait here,' she ordered, 'I'll get your salads.'

'Please, nurse,' said an old man. 'Can we have a hamburger?' Their faces lit up. 'Hamburgers,' said another old man. 'Yes, hamburgers.' They started to chant. 'Hamburgers, hamburgers, hamburgers.' Their eyes shone. Their wrinkles cracked into smiles. 'Hamburgers, hamburgers, hamburgers.'

'Stop this noise at once,' snapped the nurse. 'You'll get what you're given.' She was talking to them as if

135

they were little kids. Their smiles fell from their faces like caterpillars dropping off a tree. The nurse walked inside the shop.

'What have you got there?' said a voice. It was one of the old people. He nodded at my little robot man. He was a nice man. He told me that his name was Fred. He listened carefully while I explained. So did all the others. They gathered around and nodded and chuckled while I told them how the little robot man worked.

Fred shook his head. 'I don't like the sound of it,' he said. 'It's like trusting to luck.'

But the others were all excited. 'Try it out,' said an old man. 'Yes,' yelled someone else. 'Give us a demo.'

5

I looked up at the smiling faces. Why not? I took out my fifty dollars. 'Should I spend this?' I said aloud. I pulled the nose on the little robot man. His eyes spun. 'Green,' I yelled. 'That means yes.'

'Hamburgers,' said one crafty old guy with no teeth. 'Ask it if it wants to buy fifteen hamburgers.'

'Okay,' I said. 'Will I buy fifteen hamburgers? Yes

or no?' I pulled the little robot man's nose. The eyes turned up red. Toothless was disappointed.

'Twenty,' he screeched. 'Ask if it wants twenty hamburgers.'

'Yes, yes,' said all the others. 'Twenty hamburgers. Twenty.'

I asked the little robot man and this time his eyes turned up green. Everyone cheered. I went into the shop and bought twenty hamburgers. The nurse wasn't anywhere to be seen. I guess she must have been in the washroom.

The old folks munched into the hamburgers. They were really hungry. Some of them patted me on the back. I felt good helping all these people and giving them such a good time. Fred wouldn't take a hamburger. He just shook his head in a kindly sort of way. 'I'll wait for the salad,' he said.

'Try something else,' said Toothless. 'Ask it something else.' He started to get excited. He stared at their bus that was parked by the side of the road. 'The bus,' he said. 'Ask it if we should nick the bus.' They all started to grin wickedly with mouths full of hamburger. 'The bus,' they chanted. 'The bus, the bus, the bus.'

I wasn't so sure about this. The nurse was in

charge of the bus. But what the heck. 'Do we take the bus?' I said to the little robot man. I pulled his nose. His eyes spun. Green. It was green for yes.

The old people pushed and shoved and scrambled on the bus. 'Nick the bus,' they chuckled. 'Nick the bus.' I was swept on with the rest.

Toothless jumped into the driver's seat and started up the engine. 'I used to race cars at Phillip Island,' he chuckled. 'Five firsts and six seconds. Eleven trophies.' He let out the clutch and the bus roared off. I looked back and saw the crabby nurse run out from the hamburger joint. She was yelling and waving her fists.

Everyone cheered and waved back. Some of them made rude signs at her with their fingers. Fred sat at the back looking worried.

The bus rocketed through the traffic at enormous speed. We were approaching a T-intersection. 'Which way?' yelled Toothless. 'Left or right?'

'I don't know,' I yelled.

'Ask him,' screeched Toothless.

I pulled on the nose. 'Left,' I screamed. 'Yes or no?' The eyes rolled. The bus plummeted on. Into the intersection. Cars screeched and swerved. A brick wall seemed to rush towards us. The eyes stopped.

Red. 'Right,' I yelled. 'Turn right.'

Toothless pulled on the wheel. The bus lurched around. The tyres screamed. Blue smoke swirled through the air. We missed the brick wall by about one centimetre. Other drivers sounded their horns. Boy, were they mad. But our passengers cheered and screamed. They were loving every minute of it.

'Put my foot down? Yes or no?' yelled Toothless. The answer was green. Toothless did as he was told. He stepped on the accelerator. The bus screamed along the road. Suddenly I heard something. A police siren. The police were giving chase.

'Pull over or run for it?' yelled Toothless.

'Pull over,' said a voice. It was Fred. He leaned across and pulled out the ignition key. 'This has gone far enough,' he said. The bus bumped to a standstill and the old folk got off the bus. They were all still grinning with excitement as the police walked up.

I edged towards the back of the crowd. 'Run for it, yes or no?' I whispered. I pulled the nose and my little robot man's eyes rolled. Green. I looked for somewhere to run.

That's when I saw the crane. With the ladder straight up the side. 'The crane,' I whispered again.

'Yes or no?' I was hoping it was going to be red. But it wasn't. The eyes spun to green.

'Give me that,' said Fred. He took the little robot man from my hands and turned it over. There was a little door on its back. Fred opened the door and started to fiddle around inside. He was doing something to it.

'No,' I yelled. 'Give it back.' I snatched the little robot man from his hands.

A large policeman yelled at the crowd. 'Who's responsible for all this?' he said in a stern voice.

There was dead silence. Then Toothless turned around and pointed to me. 'Him,' he yelled. 'Him.'

I started to run. I belted along the street towards the crane. The police set out after me. And the old folk. And the nurse. 'Stop,' they screamed. 'Stop.' They yelled and called and stumbled. I fled for my life. Towards the crane.

I looked up. My legs trembled. My head felt as if it was a ball on the end of a piece of string. I didn't want to go. But the little robot man had given his orders. I put my foot on the bottom rung. And started climbing. Up, up, up. Hand over foot. Higher and higher. I looked up at the clouds. I dared not stare below.

6

So here I am. Stuck halfway up the ladder. I am too scared to go up. And too scared to climb down. The people are like little pins far beneath. I have been here for ages. My hands are getting tired. My feet are numb. If I don't do something soon I will fall. Over and over and over. Like a caterpillar falling off a leaf. Only no one will pick me up and put me back.

Someone is starting to climb up. It's hard to see so far below but I think it is Dad. What if he falls? It will be my fault. I don't know what to do. I reach for my little robot man and pull his nose. I stare at the eyes as they spin. They stop. 'Oh no,' I say. 'Oh no.'

I start to climb down to my doom. Slowly. Painfully. One foot after another without looking. I am scared I am going to fall. But I don't. Finally I get to the bottom and Dad and Mum hug me. The old people all cheer. Fred smiles at me.

The police are angry. 'He could have killed himself. Or someone else,' says the policeman.

'He's not himself today,' says Dad. 'We told him we are getting divorced. He's upset.' Mum is crying. We are all still crying when we get home.

I hope that Mum and Dad will change their minds

now. And not split up. But they don't. I still have to choose between them. Will I go interstate with Mum? Or stay with Dad? I sit on my bed and decide to give my little robot man one more go. I pull his nose. 'Green for Dad,' I say. The eyes spin. And stop. Just like they did on the crane.

I toss the little robot man out of the window and walk into the lounge-room. Mum and Dad are sitting there. 'I've made up my mind,' I yell. '*You're* getting divorced. Not me. You choose. It's your problem, not mine.' They both look at each other. They know I am right.

7

So. It all turns out to be not so bad. Mum and Dad still split up. But Mum doesn't go interstate. She rents a house in the next street. Sometimes I stay with her and sometimes I stay with Dad. I can choose whichever I like. If Dad's in a bad mood I stay with Mum for a couple of days. Then I go back. It could be a lot worse.

And the little robot man? Some passing kids find him on the footpath. It makes me smile and remember what Fred did. 'Look at this little robot,' says one of them. 'He has one green eye and one red one.'

Choosing a brilliant book
can be a tricky business...
but not any more

www.puffin.co.uk

The best selection of books at your fingertips

So get clicking!

Searching the site is easy – you'll find
what you're looking for at the click of a mouse,
from great authors to brilliant books and more!

hotnews@puffin

Hot off the press!
You'll find all the latest exclusive Puffin news here

Where's it happening?
Check out our author tours and events programme

Best-sellers
What's hot and what's not? Find out in our charts

E-mail updates
Sign up to receive all the latest news
straight to your e-mail box

Links to the coolest sites
Get connected to all the best author web sites

Book of the Month
Check out our recommended reads

www.puffin.co.uk

Choosing a brilliant book
can be a tricky business...
but not any more

www.puffin.co.uk

The best selection of books at your fingertips

So get clicking!

Searching the site is easy - you'll find
what you're looking for at the click of a mouse,
from great authors to brilliant books and more!

Everyone's got different taste . . .

I like stories that make me laugh

Animal stories are definitely my favourite

I'd say fantasy is the best

I like a bit of romance

It's got to be adventure for me

I really love poetry

I like a good mystery

Whatever you're into, we've got it covered . . .

www.puffin.co.uk

Read more in Puffin

For complete information about books available from Puffin – and Penguin – and how to order them, contact us at the appropriate address below. Please note that for copyright reasons the selection of books varies from country to country.

www.puffin.co.uk

In the United Kingdom: Please write to Dept EP, Penguin Books Ltd,
Bath Road, Harmondsworth, West Drayton, Middlesex UB7 ODA

In the United States: Please write to Penguin Putnam Inc., P.O. Box 12289,
Dept B, Newark, New Jersey 07101–5289 or call 1–800–788–6262

In Canada: Please write to Penguin Books Canada Ltd,
10 Alcorn Avenue, Suite 300, Toronto, Ontario M4V 3B2

In Australia: Please write to Penguin Books Australia Ltd,
P.O. Box 257, Ringwood, Victoria 3134

In New Zealand: Please write to Penguin Books (NZ) Ltd,
Private Bag 102902, North Shore Mail Centre, Auckland 10

In India: Please write to Penguin Books India Pvt Ltd,
11 Panscheel Shopping Centre, Panscheel Park, New Delhi 110 017

In the Netherlands: Please write to Penguin Books Netherlands bv,
Postbus 3507, NL–1001 AH Amsterdam

In Germany: Please write to Penguin Books Deutschland GmbH,
Metzlerstrasse 26, 60594 Frankfurt am Main

In Spain: Please write to Penguin Books S. A., Bravo Murillo 19,
1° B, 28015 Madrid

In Italy: Please write to Penguin Italia s.r.l.,
Via Felice Casati 20, I–20124 Milano

In France: Please write to Penguin France S. A.,
17 rue Lejeune, F–31000 Toulouse

In Japan: Please write to Penguin Books Japan, Ishikiribashi Building,
2–5–4, Suido, Bunkyo-ku, Tokyo 112

In South Africa: Please write to Longman Penguin Southern Africa (Pty) Ltd,
Private Bag X08, Bertsham 2013